Robbers in the Theatre

'You were both here all night, weren't you?'
    May shook her head wordlessly.
    'Weren't you?' repeated Nick, forcing her body
out over the fly-rail so that her feet swung clear of
the cat-walk. 'Answer me or I'll let go.'
    A wave of sickness flooded over her. The stage
hung below her at a crazy angle.
    'Yes, yes! We were here,' she sobbed.
    'Why?' he demanded. 'What were you at?'
    She had no fight left in her. What was the use?
She was about to tell him everything when
suddenly she felt arms about her waist. She was
being dragged back over the fly-rail. She heard
a thud as a fist struck Nick's body. Richie and
Mickser had arrived. Then she was lying in a
tangled heap on the cat-walk...

Carolyn Swift

Robbers in the Theatre

Illustrated by Terry Myler

ACORN BOOKS
The Children's Press

To Carl
whose recorded voice was part
of the celebration of the work
of Alan Simpson in the Olympia Theatre
on 14th September 1980

First published in 1984 by
The Children's Press
90 Lower Baggot Street, Dublin 2

© Carolyn Swift
© Illustrations The Children's Press

This book is published with the assistance of
The Arts Council (An Chomhairle Ealaíon), Ireland

ISBN 0 900068 87 6 cased
ISBN 0 900068 88 4 paper

Printed in Ireland by Mount Salus Press

Contents

Go for gold,
   The tale is told;
A worm can turn,
   And the pass is sold.
Three brass balls,
   A stranger calls;
A yellow-eyed ghost,
   And the curtain falls

1 Go for Gold

On the first day of the summer holidays, Maura Reilly set off on her bike for the North Circular Road. The bike was a gift, she thought. If she and the rest of the gang had not got bikes as a reward for discovering the treasure of St. Mary's Abbey she would have had a long walk to the North Circular Road from their little yellow-brick house beside the Four Courts, and she could not wait to see her friend Linda again.

Linda had sent her a typewritten letter from her English boarding-school telling Maura when she would be home. Typewritten letters were looked on with suspicion in Maura's home. They were usually from Dublin Corporation to point out that the rent was overdue again, but Maura knew Linda typed her letters because she was blind. In her letter Linda had written that she had exciting news and Maura was impatient to hear what it was.

So she rode fast up Church Street and through Phibsboro' until she reached the tall red-brick house with the laurel bush in the garden. It looked a lot smarter than when she and Richie had first called there hoping to earn a few pounds from a day's gardening. But then Linda's grandfather had been very ill and the sour-faced housekeeper had let the place go to rack and ruin. Now the doors and windows were freshly painted and the grass and hedges neat and tidy. There was no work for a casual gardener now, thought Maura.

Lizzie, who was now housekeeper in the place of the woman they had called Sourpuss, opened the door:

'Ah, Maura, come in! Linda's in the front room with her grand-dad. Go in and I'll put your bike out the back.

Maura could hear the sound of music coming from the front room as she left her coat down on the chair in the hall, and when she opened the door she saw that Linda was playing the piano while old Mr. Mooney sat listening in the big leather armchair. Linda stopped playing when she heard the door opening.

'Don't stop!' cried Maura. 'It sounds great.'

'Maura!' Linda exclaimed joyfully, rising from the piano stool. 'I'm so glad you've come.'

'Tell her your news, Linda,' said her grandfather, as the two girls hugged each other.

'Really, Grand-dad!' laughed Linda. 'We didn't even ask after the others yet.' And she peppered Maura with questions about her friends Richie and May Byrne, and Whacker, Imelda and Mickser.

'They're all fine,' Maura told her, 'but what's this great news?'

'Linda won first prize for piano at school,' said her grandfather. 'And next year, if she gets her exams, she may come back here and go to the College of Music.'

'Oh, that's great!' cried Maura. 'Play something for me so I can hear how good you are.'

Linda looked embarrassed: 'I'll play the Chopin piece I played at the end of term concert, if you'll do something yourself after.'

'But I can't play the piano,' said Maura.

'You can sing, can't you?' Linda retorted.

8

'Oh, I couldn't!' Singing in front of Linda's grandfather was not like singing with the others at school or just for fun, Maura thought, especially when Linda was so good at the piano.

'You must or I won't play,' Linda said. 'D'you want me to or not?'

'Of course I do,' Maura said, 'only...'

But Linda did not wait for her to finish. She began to play music that was sad and lovely at the same time, one minute making Maura want to dance and the next becoming almost creepy, reminding her of the night she had gone alone in search of Richie and Whacker and seen the moonlight striking the square tower of St. Michan's and pictured all the dead people in the crypt. It made her feel shivery and excited at the same time, so that she almost forgot to clap when Linda finished, but she knew Linda must be very good to have made her feel like that. Then she remembered that they were expecting her to sing. But what could she sing? Nothing seemed right after the music Linda had just played.

'D'you know *Danny Boy*,' Linda asked, 'because I could play that for you?'

Maura nodded. It was not the sort of song she had been thinking of, but she thought she knew the words.

'I'll try,' she said, and Linda started to play the introduction.

'Oh, Danny Boy, the pipes, the pipes are calling...' Maura began nervously, but Linda's playing made her forget all about old Mr. Mooney sitting listening to her until he applauded at the end.

'You have a nice voice,' he told her, 'sweet and true. You ought to have singing lessons.'

Maura looked at him in amazement. She had often wished her father could find another job, so her mother would be in better humour and stop working for the contract cleaners. It would be nice , too, to be able to keep the money she earned for baby-sitting or a day's cleaning, but she had never thought of spending it on anything as useless as singing lessons.

But old Mr. Mooney seemed equally amazed that she should think of singing lessons as something useless.

'If your voice was properly trained it might earn you a great deal of money,' he said.

'I dunno,' Maura said doubtfully. 'One of the lads in the Square sings with a group, but they don't get that much out of it. Not by the time it's split between the four of them and they've paid for their gear.'

'I wasn't thinking of that sort of singing,' Mr. Mooney told her.

'Grand-dad means that if you had your voice trained you could sing in concerts, or operas even.'

Maura laughed. The idea of her singing high-faluting stuff like that was funny.

'Anyway, there's no money for lessons,' she said.

'Wait a minute,' Mr. Mooney said. 'I'm sure there was something about singers being needed,' and he started turning the pages of the paper that lay across his knee. But the girls were no longer listening. Maura was trying to tell Linda everything that had happened since they last met, like Mickser's elder brother finding May and Richie's dog Patchie eating rings round him in the kitchen of the Bridge Cafe, and Whacker nearly going out of his mind because the telly broke down.

Their laughter was interrupted by Mr. Mooney,

triumphantly waving the paper at them.

'There!' he cried. 'I knew I'd seen it somewhere. They're holding auditions tomorrow morning at ten in the Olympia. Why not go along and see if they'd have something for you?'

'Oh, I couldn't!' Maura said again.

'That's what you said when I asked you to sing,' Linda pointed out, 'but you found you could.'

It was all very well for Linda, thought Maura. No one was asking her to stand up and sing in front of a crowd of strangers.

'Your mother will want you to get some sort of job for the summer, won't she?' asked Linda. 'And it would be much more fun to be singing than cleaning.'

'Of course it would,' Maura said. 'And the Olympia's only a hop and a skip from the Square. But they'd never take me.'

'You don't know that till you try,' said Mr. Mooney. 'They say here there's a large chorus.'

'If only Linda could come too, ' Maura said.

Linda laughed: 'I'd need a singing guide-dog on stage. Why don't you ask May? She might get a job too.'

Maura brightened up at that. She always felt less scared when May Byrne was with her. But when she met May in the Square that evening she just laughed:

'Even Mammy says I sing like a crow! There's no point in annoying them by trying for it.' But when she saw the look of disappointment on Maura's face she added: 'But I'll come with you for the crack if you like.'

'And where are yous two off to?' Imelda wanted to know as she joined them in time to overhear May's last sentence. On being told about the auditions she said at once that she would go too. If Linda's grandfather thought Maura Reilly, with her thin face and worn gaberdine, could get work in a show, Imelda had no doubt she could too.

At first the boys were inclined to jeer at them, but when Mickser Dolan realized there was money to be made, he changed his tune.

'If they're giving anything for it we might as well have it,' he pointed out, and Richie, May's brother, agreed:

'It could be a right bit of gas.'

'I seen a rock musical on the telly,' Imelda's brother added, and they all knew that settled it. Anything worth seeing Whacker had seen on television, so if he had seen it on television it must be worth seeing.

Next morning all six of them set out for the Olympia Theatre. Patchie wanted to go to, but May told him there was no part for a dog and he must stay and guard the house. Then they hurried along Capel Street and across the Liffey into Parliament Street. They were heading for City Hall when Whacker jerked his head in the direction of East Essex Street.

'This way,' he said.

'The Olympia's opposite the castle, stupid,' Mickser retorted.

'Stupid yerself,' said Whacker. 'We want the stage door in the lane.'

'How d'you know?' asked Maura.

'We're not gonna buy tickets, are we?' replied Whacker. 'We want the door the actors use.'

'I'd have gone to the front,' said Maura, feeling glad Whacker had come with them.

'What harm!' sniffed Mickser. 'Old Go-be-the-Wall with the brass buttons woulda told us where to go.'

When they got to the stage door it was shut, but Whacker banged on it and a man opened it. Just inside was a sort of box with a glass window and beyond that a wide corridor full of people.

'Yes?' asked the man who opened the door.

'We've come for the auditions,' said Whacker grandly, and the man stood back and let them in.

'Wait there with the others,' he told them. 'There'll be someone along to you in a minute.'

Maura plucked at May's sleeve as they joined the crowd of people. 'D'you think these are all up for it too?' she whispered.

May nodded: 'We'll be here all day by the looks of it.'

A girl in glasses with a notebook and pencil hurried over to them and took their names and addresses.

'Your names will be called out when it's your turn,' she said. 'Have you brought your music?'

They all looked at her blankly.

'The sheet music of what you're going to sing — for the accompanist to play from,' she explained wearily. She had a great many people to deal with.

The others turned on Maura accusingly.

'It didn't say anything about that on the paper,' she stammered.

'You can hardly expect her to play without music, can you?' the girl snapped, starting to turn away from them.

Maura had supposed they would ask her to sing something from the show. Now she realized they would never have time to teach everyone a new tune. She felt terribly stupid.

'I'm sorry,' she mumbled. 'I didn't know.'

The girl's face softened a little.

'What was it you wanted to sing?' she asked.

'Danny Boy,' Maura whispered, because it was the first thing she thought of.

'She'll probably manage that for you all right,' the girl said. 'D'you know your key?'

Maura shook her head.

'Oh well, I daresay we can give you a second or two to sort it out,' she said. 'What about the rest of you?' adding as they hesitated, 'You can either pick something well known or go and get the music. If you haven't sorted it out by the time the names are called I'm afraid you're out.'

May stepped forward: 'You needn't bother calling my name. I can't sing. I only came with the others.'

The girl cast her eyes to heaven and struck May's name off the list, saying: 'If you're not auditioning you'd better go. We've quite enough cluttering up the place as it is.' And she turned to the man in the queue behind them, who at once held out his music.

'A professional at last,' they heard her say. 'Some of these amateurs would drive you round the bend.'

'I'm sorry, Maura,' May said. 'I'd better go. Don't let anyone put you down,' and she gave Maura's arm an encouraging squeeze before fighting her way back through the people who had crowded in after them, until she reached the box with the glass window.

As she got to it, the man came out and opened the stage door to let in a woman about the same age as May's mother. May stood aside for her to pass and then recognized her.

14

'Hullo, Mrs. Mullen,' she said.

'Well, if it isn't May Byrne,' the woman said, surprised. 'Your Auntie Lil was only talking about you last night, saying she hadn't seen hair nor hide of any of you for she didn't know how long!'

'Mammy's been awful busy lately, Mrs. Mullen,' May told her. 'And it's a long way to Ballyfermot.'

'And the bus fares all up again,' Mrs. Mullen agreed. 'But what are you doing here?'

'I came down with the others,' May started to explain, but her voice was drowned by the babble of voices from the waiting crowd.

'I can't hear a word you're saying, child,' Mrs. Mullen said, 'Come on up to the Wardrobe and tell me all the news, so I can tell your Aunt Lil and Uncle Jack when I go home tonight.' And she hurried May up the stairs to the floor above and into a room where piles of brightly coloured materials lay on a table beside a sewing-machine and an ironing-board stood under the window.

'D'you work here then?' May asked in surprise, as Mrs. Mullen took off her coat and hung it on a rail beside a row of dresses.

'For the best part of six months now,' Mrs. Mullen said, 'but this musical will be the biggest thing I've tackled yet. There's a stack of costumes to be made for it. I've told them they'll have to take on extra help for the run . But you never said what you're doing here.'

'Six of us came lookin' for work,' May explained, 'only Mammy says the old cat has more notes in her head than I have!'

'How are you with a needle?' Mrs. Mullen asked

suddenly, as she took the cover off the sewing-machine.

May looked up sharply.

'I never done any dress-makin', she said. 'Only let down hems and stitched on buttons and mended young Brendan's gansey when he ripped it.'

But Mrs. Mullen did not seem in the least put out.

'Are you any good with an iron?' she asked.

'Mammy says I press her dress good as the cleaners,' May said. 'But I'd never be able for makin' costumes.'

'What harm!' Mrs. Mullen said. 'I've another girl who can sew, but I need someone to fetch and carry and run messages. If you can press and tack and stitch headbands and sew on press-fasteners you'll do me.'

'You mean, you could give me a job?' May asked, excited. That way she would be part of the show even if she could not sing.

'Of course, I'll have to have a word with them in the office first,' Mrs. Mullen said. 'Can you call back after your dinner?'

'Oh yes, Mrs. Mullen, and thanks a lot!'

'Not at all, child. I'll be only too glad to have someone I can really rely on. Some of the young ones that are going today are real giddy. You'd never know would they even turn up!'

May ran down the stairs in a rush to tell Maura the good news, but Maura had disappeared. There was no sign of the others either. Then the girl with glasses came out of a door beside the stage door.

May slipped back into the darkness of the stairs, for fear she would be scolded for still being there, until the girl disappeared through another door opposite the first. Before it swung shut behind her, May heard the faint sound of *Danny Boy* coming from somewhere on the far side. Greatly daring, she crept to the door and opened it an inch or two.

Just in front of her in the half-light was a heavy cloth that ran up into the darkness above, leaving only a narrow passage to right and left. She tiptoed to the corner and peeped around a black curtain hanging in front.

Maura was standing on the stage in a pool of light, facing out into a black void that May guessed must be where the audience would sit. Behind her was the front of a cottage though there was no proper back to it, and behind that again a wall against a wide expanse of blue representing the sky. At the same time she realized it was the front of the cloth she had just walked around and guessed it must be the scenery for the show that would be on in the theatre that night. Out of the blackness below came the sound of a piano but May could neither see it nor who was playing it.

Maura'a voice seemed to soar up and up like a bird and then suddenly drop in a sad little fall, before dying away in a hush that seemed to last for ages. Then a woman's voice called something out of the blackness. Maura put up a hand to shade her eyes from the lights shining down on her. A man scrambled up on to the stage and went over to her. He was short with a thin face, lank black hair and eyes that darted this way and that.

'She wants to know can you come back tomorrow at eleven?' he said.

Maura nodded, bewildered.

'Well, get going then,' he said, pushing her over towards where May stood. 'There's others here beside you, you know.'

'I'm sorry,' Maura said meekly.

'And you needn't look like someone nicked your iced lolly,' he added. 'Didn't you get what you came for?'

'You mean there's a job for me?' Maura asked, hardly daring to breathe.

'D'you think they want you back tomorrow to throw sugar at you?' and he turned back into the darkness shouting: 'Next!'

A man walked out from the far side into the pool of light and May caught sight of the girl with glasses bending over the edge of the stage, holding out a sheet of music. Then she was hugging Maura in the half-light behind the black velvet curtains.

On the way home May told Maura that she too had a chance of a job and Maura was even more excited at the thought of them both working together in that strange mysterious place where everything was so new and unexpected. Then May remembered the others.

'What happened Imelda and the lads?' she asked.

Maura giggled: 'Poor Whacker! He went on bold as brass and sang *The Knock Song,* without the piano or anything, and they called out, "Thank you!" before he'd got half-way through it. They wouldn't let him finish it even. He was ragin'! He really fancies himself singin' that after the way everyone cheered him at the party.'

'He shoulda known this was different,' May said. 'How about the others?'

'Well, Richie said if it was a rock musical they oughta sing a rock number, but the pianist didn't know any of the things he wanted to sing, so in the heel of the hunt they all sang, *Any Dream Will Do?* outa *Joseph and the*

Technicolour Dreamcoat.'

'Imelda too?' asked May. 'But that's a man's song.'

'I don't think they cared,' Maura said. 'You could sing any old thing. They just wanted to know what your voice was like.'

'And did they get anything?'

'They said they'd let them know. I think it depends on how good the others are.'

'Then why did they ask you to come back?'

'I dunno,' Maura said. 'I suppose we'll only have to wait till tomorrow to find out.'

After dinner May went back to the theatre to hear she was to start on Monday as temporary Junior Wardrobe Assistant.

'Did he say anything to you about Liverpool?' Mrs. Mullen wanted to know when May stuck her head into the room at the top of the stairs to tell her it was all arranged. May shook her head.

'The old skinflint probably thinks he'll pick up someone over there to save paying maintenance, but he's another think coming. With a wardrobe this size I'll need someone who knows the run of the show.'

'You mean the show's going to Liverpool?'

'After the Dublin run finishes,' Mrs. Mullen told her. 'But you can tell your mother I'll mind you. You get touring rates and you can share rooms with me. If she's bothered I'll talk to her myself.'

'Ah, it'll probably be all right if I'm with you.' May said. 'But I don't know about Maura.'

'Maura?' Mrs. Mullen looked puzzled.

'My friend who auditioned this morning,' May explained. 'I doubt her Mammy'd let her leave Dublin.'

'Say nothing to her till she's offered a contract,' Mrs. Mullen advised. 'In this business you can be sure of nothing till you have it in writing.'

May nodded, but that night she could not sleep for worrying about it. But she was sure Mrs. Reilly would never let Maura sing in a show if it meant leaving home. She had even tried to stop her going to Ballinascorney the time the bank robbers hid out on Larry Keogh's farm. Maura was going to be terribly disappointed. May was still trying to think what to say to Mrs. Reilly when she fell asleep.

2   The Tale is Told.

After breakfast next morning, May ran across the Square and knocked on the door of Danny Noonan's house. The old sailor smiled when he saw her.

'And what brings you calling on an old man this fine day?' he asked.

'Did you ever hear tell of the *Táin*, Danny?' May asked in turn.

'Deed and I did,' Danny said. 'Isn't the *Táin* one of the great tales from long ago?'

'That's what they told me at the theatre, so I was certain you'd know all about it,' May said, for since Danny gave up going to sea on account of his arthritis he had spent most of his time reading and knew more tales than anyone else. 'Will you tell me about it, Danny?'

'I will, of course,' the old man replied, 'but it's not a tale can be told in a minute, so you'd best come in,' and he led the way into the little front parlour that was full of the things he had brought back from his voyages, like the dried starfish and the two huge shells he had picked up on a Pacific island beach and a curious curved sword he had bought in an old shop in Istanbul.

'Tell me this and tell me no more,' he said, as he sat himself stiffly down in the chair beside the window. 'What put you in mind of the *Táin*?'

'Well,' May told him, 'I got the offer of a job, only before I say anything to Mammy I thought I oughta find out everything I could about it.'

'That would be the right and proper thing to do,' the old man agreed. 'But what has the job to do with the *Táin*?'

'I'd be helpin' out on costumes for a show in the Olympia, *The Black and White Bullfight*,' May explained, 'and when I asked them what it was about they said it was a rock musical made outa the *Táin*. What is the *Táin*, Danny?'

'The *Táin Bó Cúailnge* is its real name,' said Danny. '*The Cattle Raid of Cooley* 'twould be in English. The story goes that one night Ailill, King of Connacht, and his wife, Queen Maeve, had a right diggin' match. You see, a daughter of the High King of Ireland the likes of Maeve would bring a power of things in her dowry when she married, from gold and jewellery to pots and pans, and from fine clothes and servants to sheep and horses and pigs and cattle. So Maeve started givin' out that Ailill was a great deal better off on account of all the things she brought with her when she married.

'Of course,' he went on, 'a brother of the King of Leinster, the likes of Ailill, wasn't going to agree to that, so he told Maeve that what she'd brought with her was

21

only a spit in the ocean to what he already had. Well, one thing led to another until nothing would do them only go through each and every mortal thing they owned to see who had the most.'

'Wouldn't you think kings and queens would have more sense?' May said, as Danny paused to relight his pipe, but he only shook his head.

'No one was ever a whit the wiser for being better off,' he said. 'Howinever, it turned out that the pair of them had the very same of everything, whether it was rings or servants or buckets or cows. Except for one thing...'

He paused dramatically.

'What was that?' May asked, as he knew she would

'A bull with white horns that was in the King's herd,' he answered. 'And there wasn't his like anywhere else in the whole kingdom.'

'I bet Maeve was ragin',' said May.

'She was,' said Danny, 'and in the end didn't she decide to ask for the lend of a loan of a brown bull that was in Ulster and said to be the equal of the white-horned bull, if not even better.'

'And did she get it?' asked May.

'She did not,' Danny replied, 'Maybe she would have only for the messengers she sent to ask for it took a drop too much to drink and let out that if they didn't get the permission they'd rob the bull anyways.'

'The eejits!' May cried.

'You can say that again,' Danny agreed, 'for in the heel of the hunt such a diggin' match started over the head of it that the men of Ulster and the men of Connacht went to war.'

'Over nothing worse nor an old bull?' May gasped.

22

'That's a fact,' said Danny, 'and there's many a country today that'd go to war over as little. Howinever, Ailill and Maeve led the men of Connacht against the forces of King Conor Mac Nessa and the great Ulster warrior Cúchulainn and they fought a power of battles. Maeve and Ailill were gettin' the worst of it so they started talkin' about makin' a truce, and then what d'ye think happened?'

'I dunno,' May said.

'The two bulls decided to settle the matter themselves, and they fought for days and days up and down the length and breadth of Ireland, and in the end the white-horned bull of Connacht was killed and the brown bull of Ulster carried his dead body back home to Ulster on his horns.'

'So Ulster won?' May said.

'I'd say they did,' Danny said, 'though the brown bull was scarcely back home before he died too from the terrible wounds he got in the fighting.'

'Well,' said May. 'I dunno how they're gonna made a musical outa that!'

'No more do I,' Danny said. 'But it's great all the same that it's one of our own tales they're tellin' this time, instead of something that happened in America or France or on the other side of the world.'

'I think maybe I'll only tell Mammy it's about Ireland long ago,' May said, but what she was really thinking was that nothing Danny had told her was going to help one bit with talking to Mrs. Reilly.

And yet, as it happened, she need not have worried at all. When Maura came back from seeing the business manager at the theatre she was in a daze. Instead of getting work in the chorus as she had hoped, she had been offered a proper part. True it was only a very small one, as maid servant to Queen Maeve, but she would be singing a few lines all by herself. This meant that she would be getting more money, and although even then it was not a great deal it would be her very first weekly wage.

'They don't pay you by the hour like for the cleanin' or the baby-sittin',' she told May. 'They give you money for the week no matter when you work.'

May looked wise: 'Mrs. Mullen says that's because they work you so hard it'd cost them a packet to pay you by the hour! Have you told yer mother yet?'

Maura nodded.

'At first she thought I was only lettin' on,' she said, 'but when she heard I'd be getting a weekly wage for the whole summer she was real pleased.'

'She doesn't mind about you going to Liverpool then?'

'Not when I said I'd be getting extra and I'd be with you and Mrs. Mullen the whole time,' Maura told her.

So it was all going to happen, May thought!

Next day Imelda, Richie and Mickser were offered work too. It was only in the chorus and when he heard how little they would be paid Mickser at first said he was going to turn it down, but in the end the thought of being able to tell them all about it in school was too much for him. Besides, as he said to the others: ' Being paid for doin' nothing only singin' is money for old rope and a lot easier than gardenin'!'

'Poor old Whacker,' said Maura to Imelda on Sunday morning, as May finished telling them the story of the

24

Táin as Danny had told it to her. 'He must feel terrible left out.'

'I don't think he's one bit bothered.' Imelda said. 'He's talkin' about nothing only the woman he saw on the *Late Late* last night. Some big Hollywood star, he said she was, and all hung over with diamonds the size of twopenny pieces.'

'And is she here in Ireland?' asked Maura.

'Of course she is, stupid,' said Imelda, 'How else would Gay Byrne be talking to her? She's gonna be in a film they're makin' here in August. Whacker says the old musical's only buttons beside a big film and he'll maybe get work on that as an extra.'

'I wouldn't doubt him,' said Maura. When Whacker made up his mind to go after something he nearly always got it. She decided he must never have been really interested in the musical.

May's thoughts were different. It was a new experience for Whacker to be left out of anything. He might just be trying to keep his end up, but she kept her thoughts to herself.

A week later, Imelda, Richie and Mickser felt Whacker had the laugh on them after all. Being in the chorus was anything but money for old rope. They had, in fact, never worked so hard in all their lives. Again and again the chorus master made them go over every phrase. They were rehearsing in a cold church hall a long way from the theatre; there were no bright lights or colourful costumes; and the actors and actresses playing Maeve, Ailill, Conor and Cúchulainn were nowhere to be seen.

'We were conned!' Mickser said in disgust, as they

tramped home one evening exhausted.

'Yeah,' said Richie, 'but don't let on to Whacker. We don't want him crowin' over us.'

They had been working all day on the same song and did not even know how it fitted into the story.

'May was the cute one, not even goin' for it, 'Imelda said. 'Now she's in the theatre all day, seein' everything that goes on.'

May would probably have agreed with her. She loved the bright, glittering costumes that were beginning to pile up on the hangers and the monotonous work of stitching headbands and sewing press-studs was brightened by the people who came in for costume fittings. Most of all she loved to be sent in search of the designer to show her a sample of material or collect more of the little drawings she did of the costumes they were to make. That gave May the excuse to peep in at the rehearsals on stage, where the real action was. The only thing she did not like about her job was Scruffy.

Scruffy, of course, was not her real name. Mrs. Mullen called her Betty, but May thought of her as Scruffy from the very first day, because that was exactly how she looked. Her straw-like hair was a mess, as if it had once been cut in punk style and then left to grow out. In the same way, she seemed to have once had a pink streak in it, but that too was nearly grown out and now just made her hair look funny. She wore a loose grey sweater with inkstains on it that had gone into holes under the arms, and, instead of jeans, she wore a denim skirt with the hem ripped and hanging down on one side. Her finger-nails were all bitten and May felt her hands should have a good scrub before she touched the beautiful shiny materials. But as soon as she began to sew her movements were no longer awkward. The needle flew in and out of the cloth as she stitched what looked to May like diamonds, emeralds and rubies on the headbands and facings of the cloaks.

'Are they awfully expensive?' May asked.

'Woolworth's best,' snapped Scruffy. 'You must be a right gorm if you think we'd use the real stuff.'

'Nothing's what it seems in the theatre,' Mrs. Mullen nodded. 'Even the wine's only raspberry cordial and gravy browning.'

'And if I had anything valuable I'd take good care not to bring it in here,' sniffed Scruffy. 'It wouldn't be long before it was nicked.'

'You wouldn't want to be leaving your week's wages down out of your hand anyway,' Mrs. Mullen agreed. 'There's too many wandering around.'

'Thanks for the warning,' May said, and stitched in silence till it was time to go home. But next morning, arriving before the others, she could not resist peeping into the little cardboard box where Scruffy kept the coloured stones. They really did look like real jewels, she thought, holding the pieces up to the light to see them sparkle. Just then Scruffy came in and flew at her.

'How dare you meddle with my things!' she shouted. 'You keep your nose outa my business, or you'll be sorry!'

'They're only old bits of glass,' May protested. 'What harm was I doin'?'

'Poking and prying into things that don't concern you. You stick to your job and leave me do mine, or I'll tell Mrs. Mullen I caught you using her good cutting-out scissors.'

'I was only lookin',' May said, but after that she kept well out of Scruffy's way and only talked when Mrs. Mullen was there.

Maura, on the other hand, was just beginning to find her tongue. At first she had been far too much in awe of everyone around her, especially of the actress playing Queen Maeve. Maura had seen her before on television, and whenever she was around it was hard to look at anyone else. She was usually in the centre of a little group of admiring people, and was one minute keeping them all in fits of laughter and the next would round suddenly on someone in a rage that made her eyes flash. That was how the real Queen Maeve must have been, Maura thought, with the men of Connacht around her. They, too, were probably scared of arousing her anger. So Maura only spoke to her when spoken to, and then only said, 'Fine, thanks Sylvia' or 'Sorry, Sylvia,' as the case might be.

Roger, the actor who played Ailill, was much less alarming. He had several times spoken to Maura in a friendly way, even asking if she agreed that he should be standing when he told Maeve he had never before heard of a kingdom run by a woman. But Maura felt when he looked at her it was only to see how he looked in her eyes, like someone looking into a mirror and, as he only talked about himself, she never had to do more than nod her head in agreement.

Yet even Roger and Sylvia took orders from the young woman whose voice Maura had first heard coming out of the darkness after she had sung *Danny Boy*. When Maura first saw her, she could hardly

28

believe she was the director, the one who told them all where to stand and when to move. She was so slight and swift in her movements that Maura thought at first she could not be much older than herself but when she spoke she seemed so sure of herself that Maura knew she must be older than she looked. She was nice, Maura decided, but, even though everyone called her Jane, she was like one of the teachers at school and Maura could not imagine chatting to her.

The only person she really could talk to as yet was the girl with the glasses who had written down their names when they came for the audition. Maura thought now that she was not at all like the rather bossy lady she had seemed then. In fact, she was bossed around by everyone else and was expected to do so many things at once that Maura felt quite sorry for her. Her name was Phil, and she told Maura she was the assistant stage manager.

While Maura waited for her scene to be rehearsed, she would sit in the front row of seats where Phil crouched over a big book in which she wrote down all the director's instructions against the words the actors spoke. From watching her and asking questions, Maura began to learn what everyone's job was and how they turned the words on the page into the magic that gripped everyone when the lights finally went down and the great curtain went up on the finished show. But, like May, Maura, too, had one small cloud hanging over her otherwise star-filled world, and that was Nick Clarke.

Nick was the man who had come up on stage after her audition and told her to get going, and Maura now knew that he was the stage manager. He had made her feel uneasy right from the start, the way his eyes darted this way and that without ever quite meeting hers, but she knew now that he was a most important man to keep in with, for Nick could make life easier in all sorts of little ways if he liked you.

'Be an angel,' Maura had heard Sylvia say, turning the full warmth of her smile on him, 'and make sure the curtain comes down really fast on that scene. I don't want to be left with egg on my face!' And Nick would grin and wink and say: 'Leave it to me, Syl. The job's oxo!' So when Maura had to ask a favour of him she intended to be extra polite.

She was rehearsing the scene where she had to bring Maeve a cup of wine and she pretended to carry it to where Maeve lay back on her bed.

'You'll need both hands, Maura,' the director called out. 'It's not like a tea-cup, you know,' and Sylvia added in a friendly way: 'You should ask Nick to get you a substitute prop to rehearse with.'

'What's a substitute prop?' Maura whispered to Phil when she came off stage, and Phil explained that it was something more-or-less the same shape and size and weight as the thing she would be using, so she could learn how best to hold and carry it. So, after rehearsal, when she saw Nick with a pile of boxes at the side of the stage, she went over to him.

'Nick!' Maura said softly, but he was absorbed in what he was doing and never even looked up. 'Nick!' she repeated more loudly, and heard a gasp of suppressed laughter from behind her.

Nick looked up and his face was like a thundercloud.

'If you're talking to me, the name's Jimmy,' he

snapped. 'And you'd better stand outa my way if you don't want one of these on your toes!'

It came to Maura in a flash that he would not think twice about dropping one of the heavy cases on to her toes by-mistake-on-purpose, as Whacker always said, and she ran for the stage door, almost falling over Phil who was standing backstage, her hand over her mouth to stifle her laughter.

'Did you not know his name isn't really Nick?' Phil asked between giggles.

'How would I?' cried Maura. 'Isn't that what everyone calls him?'

'Not to his face,' Phil said. 'Though he must know we all call him that.'

'But why?' Maura asked. 'Why call him Nick if his name's Jimmy?'

Phil giggled again: 'Because they say he nicks everything that isn't nailed down! I don't know if it's true, but things do have a way of disappearing whenever he's around.'

When May got back to the Square that evening, the first person she saw was Whacker coming towards her, waving a newspaper.

'Did you hear the news?' he asked, as he caught up with her.

May shook her head.

'Remember the big Hollywood star was on the *Late Late* last week? The wan that's makin' the fillum here next month?'

'I remember you goin' on about her,' May replied.

'Well,' Whacker announced importantly. 'She's had

all her jewellery nicked. All them big diamonds she wore on the *Late Late,* and emeralds and rubies and everything!'

It did not seem very important to May. That sort of thing was always happening to film stars.

'It's all here on the paper,' Whacker said. 'She's in a terrible state over it.'

'Can't she buy more if she's as rich as you say?'

'She says they've great sentimental value. Her third husband gave them to her. That's why she brought them with her.'

'They were nicked in Dublin then?' May asked.

'Outa her hotel in O'Connell Street last night,' Whacker said. 'A real slick job it was and they worth thousands. The fuzz are gone mad altogether over it.'

'They're only wastin' their time,' May said. 'Whoever took them knew what he was at.'

'I dunno,' said Whacker. 'It says here they'll never be able to sell them. Not great big rocks like that.'

'Don't you know they'll have them outa the country by now,' said May. 'Isn't that the way they always do it.'

'The fuzz have all the ports and airports watched,' Whacker told her. 'They're even keepin' an eye on fishin' boats right around the country. And they've pictures of the jewellery in all the papers, the way everyone'll know what to look for.'

May took the paper he held out to her and as she glanced at the photo beneath the big black headlines, she felt a sudden shiver of excitement. It was only chance, of course, but the precious stones in the picture looked to her just like the bits of coloured glass in Scruffy's little box.

3 *A Worm Can Turn*

Next day, pressing tunics in the Wardrobe, May could not take her eyes off the gems that winked and flashed in the sunlight as Scruffy stitched them on to the neckband of Cúchulainn's cloak. Most of the costumes were by now almost ready and hung in bright colours along the rail of the press by the door. Mrs. Mullen, who was checking the list to see what still had to be done, suddenly looked up in surprise.

'Are we still short four chorus boys' tunics?' she asked. 'I thought you were seeing to them, Betty?'

Scruffy looked up, and May noticed she looked even scruffier that usual.

'I'll do them today,' she said. 'They won't take long.'

'Why don't you let May finish off those old stones?' Mrs. Mullen asked. 'It's a fairly straightforward job.'

A pink flush showed on Scruffy's sallow cheeks.

'It's my job,' she said sharply.

'It certainly has been until now, 'Mrs. Mullen agreed, startled at the anger in Scruffy's voice, 'but May could do it and she couldn't cut out those tunics. I'd do them myself only Sylvia's coming in this morning for her final fitting and I've still her ceremonial cloak to finish.'

'There's no need,' Scruffy replied sullenly. 'They'll be done.'

The strange thing, May thought, was that Scruffy did not seem to be much further on than she had been the day before, when there were hardly any stones left in her little box. And yet, when May had arrived that morning Scruffy was already in her usual place, stitching away, an overflowing ashtray at her elbow, as if she had been there for hours. How had she fallen so far behind when she worked at such speed?

Just then Nick stuck his head in the door and, without a word, Scruffy jumped up and left the room.

'What's eating her?' Mrs. Mullen asked, as soon as the door closed behind her.

'I think maybe she's tired,' May said. 'Did you see the way her eyes were sort of sunk into her head like she was up late or somethin'?'

'If she was, I bet it was on account of that Nick,' Mrs. Mullen sniffed. 'That's a friendship won't do her one bit of good.'

'You mean, Nick's her boy-friend?' May asked, surprised. 'I never knew that.'

'Nor did I till the other day,' Mrs. Mullen said. 'I never saw her with a fella before but they were in the Granary bar between the shows on Saturday and I saw them leaving the theatre together more than once during the week.'

May found it hard to think of Scruffy as anyone's girl-friend, but Nick was a bit of a weirdo too. Now that Mrs. Mullen had set her thinking, she remembered that the only time she had gone home before Scruffy she had passed Nick climbing the stairs as she left, but before she could tell Mrs. Mullen, Scruffy slammed sullenly back into the room.

Not long after that Sylvia came in for her fitting. Apart from the position of one small tuck, everything seemed to fit perfectly and she was delighted with the huge imitation emerald on her cloak.

'I feel just like Liz Taylor,' she said. 'Pity it's not the real thing.'

'What would you do if it was?' Mrs. Mullen asked, her mouth full of pins as she adjusted the tuck.

'Run away to the South of France and spend the rest of my life having a ball on the proceeds,' Sylvia laughed. 'Can't you picture me on the beach at Cannes or queening it in the Casino?'

'I think it'd be awful boring after a bit,' May said.

Sylvia turned to her sharply so that the cloak swept a little pile of pins off the table on to the floor.

'You're Maura's friend, aren't you?' she asked. 'You've a lot more to say for yourself than little mouse Maura.'

'Maura's no mouse,' May said, stoutly defending her friend. 'She's only shy.'

'Shy or no she's a lovely voice,' Sylvia said. 'I think she's going to be quite good.'

May could hardly wait to tell Maura what Sylvia had said, for Maura seemed to be getting more and more nervous as the opening night drew near, and May was half afraid her voice would shake with fear during the performance, the way it did when her mother and father had one of their big rows.

She hurried off in search of her as soon as she was finished for the day, but there was no one on stage. In the glare of the scene dock Phil was sorting props, but in answer to May's query she said Maura had already left. Then May remembered she had left her comb in the Wardrobe.

As she reached to get it down from the shelf by the mirror, she caught sight of Scruffy's little box. It must be empty now, she thought, for Scruffy had at last finished sewing on the gems and, before she had left, had started on the last of the boy's tunics. Yet, as May took the comb, she brushed the box with her wrist and heard a rattle of stones inside. Curiosity got the better of her and, almost before she knew it, she had the box in her hands and was lifting the lid.

Then she gave a gasp of surprise because the box was almost full, Red and green stones and stones as clear as diamonds glinted back at her out of the box. It was not possible, May thought! Yesterday morning, when she had seen Scruffy take a stone from it, it had been almost empty. Now it was almost full! It made no sense.

Then a terrible suspicion crept into her mind. Supposing these were the jewels that had been stolen? May felt ashamed of her thoughts. It was true that Scruffy had never been very nice to her, but that did not make her a thief. And anyway she had had the stones before ever the jewels had been stolen. Besides, a thief would never leave them where someone else might so easily find them. Had not Scruffy herself said she would never leave anything valuable in the theatre?

Then May had an idea. With so many stones in the box Scruffy would never miss one The old man in the pawnbrokers in Capel Street would tell her what it was worth. Quickly she slipped a large green stone, just like the one on Sylvia's cloak, into her pocket with her comb, put the box back on the shelf and ran from the room.

She breathed a sigh of relief when she saw the shutters were not yet over the window beneath the three golden balls which hung out over the street to show that, as well as selling jewellery, Mr. Leventon would lend money in return for articles pledged. Old Mr. Leventon himself was behind the counter when she went in. His father and his father before him had had the little shop in Capel Street. He remembered the days when the women living around the markets would bring in a clock or a christening mug every Monday and get it out again on the Friday after their husbands had been paid. It was a way of life he had thought gone for ever, but, now there were so many unemployed, some of those same women's daughters that had never before been to the pawn would sometimes slip in, shamefaced, looking for a loan on an engagement ring.

Maura's mother, rather than be seen to go herself, had once or twice sent Maura to him on a message of this sort and, as May had been with her, she knew the old man slightly. He recognized her too and smiled at her.

'And what can I do for you?' he asked, for she had not got the usual shopping bag or telltale brown paper parcel concealing the silver-plated spoons or forks that had been somebody's wedding present.

'Can you tell me, please,' May asked, 'is this a real emerald?' and she slipped the big green stone that was the twin of the one on Sylvia's cloak out of her pocket and put it down on the counter in front of the old man.

He took it up in his fingers, smiling, and turned it in the light. Then, more to please May than from any real need, he twisted a little glass into one eye and peered at the stone through it. Then, taking the glass out again, he shook his head gently.

'I'm afraid not, chicken,' he said. 'It's only coloured

glass. I'm sorry.'

'I'm not,' May said, laughing with relief. 'I don't know what I woulda done if it had been real. Thanks Mr. Leventon,' and she set out for the Square with a light heart. Now she could tell Maura the nice things Sylvia had said about her without this worry at the back of her mind.

Richie, Mickser and Imelda were also on their way home. It had been their last day in the north-side rehearsal hall. Next morning they would be rehearsing on the Olympia stage with the rest of the cast, and they were looking forward to seeing the show through from beginning to end so they could follow the story. It would be great, too, to be out of the bleak rehearsal hall which echoed to the sound of their voices. But the chorus master, eager to impress the director, had worked them even harder than usual, and they hardly spoke to each other as they crossed Malboro' Street. When they reached the chipper, Richie finally spoke:

'Have any of yous any money?'

The smell of frying potatoes made their noses twitch, and they were more than ready for a break. Between them they had the price of a single chips and they joined the small queue at the counter, their mouths watering at the sound of chips sizzling and spluttering as the great wire basket was plunged into the boiling oil.

As they stood waiting, two men thrust their way and sat down at one of the tables along the wall. Richie felt he had seen one of them before. He was still trying to place him when the man said:

'I don't like this waiting.'

He was a nasty-looking character, Richie decided. He

was heavily built with arms like a gorilla they had seen the time they went to the zoo, and he had a scar running down his left cheek. The smaller man's eyes flickered to right and left as if he was afraid someone behind him was about to pounce on him.

'Maybe you don't,' he said, 'but you gotta stay away from the theatre.'

The minute he heard his voice, Richie remembered where he had seen him before. After their auditions, it was he who had told them they would let them know. 'Don't call us, we'll call you,' he had said grinning.

The other man was speaking again:

'Don't try anything on, that's all. I'd get you, no matter how far you ran.'

The small man rolled the whites of his eyes in fear.

'Go easy, Slasher!' he pleaded. 'You can trust me.' The Adam's apple danced up and down in his throat as the man he called Slasher put a hand on his shoulder.

'I trust no one,' he said. 'Just remember that! And I'll be on that Liverpool boat along with you. You'll never be out of my sight.'

It was like something you'd see on the telly, Richie thought. He was so busy straining his ears to hear what they were saying that it was not until Mickser gave him a kick on the shins that he realized the man behind the counter had asked what he wanted. He ordered the single chips and, as the man scooped them up, glanced back at the two men. The waitress was taking their order. Paying for the chips, he followed the others out of the shop.

Later, at his tea, Richie thought about the two men in the chipper. A lot of funny things went on these days and it was best not to get mixed up in anything that did not concern you. He would have put the whole thing out of his head but for the fact that they had mentioned the theatre. Now that he knew who the man with the shifty eyes and big Adam's apple was, the theatre had to be their theatre. It struck him that May had been working there for the past two weeks. She would be able to tell him something about the man.

He waited till their parents went into the parlour to watch telly, leaving them washing the delph. Then he asked her about him.

'You mean Nick?' she asked, scraping the rasher rinds off her father's plate into Patchie's bowl. 'Maura sees more of him than me. I'm goin' round to her place soon as I've finished this. I'll ask her about him if you like. What d'you wanta know?'

'Everything,' Richie said. 'I'd come with you only I said I'd see Whacker.'

'You couldn't talk to her properly there anyways,' May pointed out. 'You know the way her mother is.'

'Get her to come back with you,' Richie suggested.

May nodded: 'See you in the Square then.'

Whacker and Richie had always hung around together, but since the day of the audition, Richie could think of nothing to talk about but the happenings of the day, like Mickser coming in a bar too soon in *That Maeve War,* and then trying to pretend it was not him. But Whacker did not want to know about rehearsals and this put a strain on the friendship. So Richie was glad that this evening he had something else to tell him. And Whacker had been interested at once.

'I bet you they've pulled off some job and Slasher's

afraid the little man might try to double-cross him,' he said.

'That's the way it sounded right enough,' Richie agreed. 'That's why I asked May to get Maura. She knows him.'

May had some difficulty persuading Maura to come.

'I don't want anything to do with it,' she said. 'The run-through is tomorrow, and I've enough to worry about without them two makin' trouble.'

She went all the same. She knew if she did not Imelda would be only too quick to suggest she was scared, so she told them all she knew about Nick, including what Phil had said about his taking anything that wasn't nailed down.

'It fits,' Whacker said. 'The way I see it, they've nicked something and yer man is takin' it across to England on the Liverpool boat.'

'Maybe when the show moves to Liverpool,' Maura suggested.

'And Slasher's afraid he won't get his share, so he's goin' with him,' Richie added.

'But the show doesn't go to Liverpool for weeks,' May objected. 'Why wait till then?'

'Because Nick has to stay with the show,' Maura said.

'But Slasher hasn't,' Richie pointed out. 'Why doesn't he take whatever it is to England himself? Then he wouldn't have to worry about Nick double-crossing him.'

Suddenly Whacker let out a yell. His face was alight with excitement.

'I know what it is,' he said. 'It's the jewels nicked offa that woman on the *Late Late*. They said on the telly that the fuzz was watchin' all the ports and airports to stop them bein' took outa the country. So they're gonna take them out with the gear from the show.'

May felt a funny cold feeling in her stomach. If Scruffy was in on it too it would explain everything. Except for one thing.

'But the jewels are only fake,' she said. 'I took one down to the pawn in Capel Street this evening to check.'

'Come again?' Whacker said.

She told them the whole story then; about Scruffy and the stones and her suspicions, and she showed them the big green emerald that was still in the pocket of her jeans. Whacker let out a whistle.

'That's just like the one on the telly!' he said.

'Then she's only coddin the people,' May said. 'For Mr. Leventon says it's only coloured glass.'

'Maybe she's trying to do the insurance,' suggested Richie.

Whacker shook his head.

'She had the stuff insured for thousands,' he said. 'And they would never have insured it without seein' it first.'

'Maybe she pulled a stroke herself,' Richie said. 'Like havin' copies made. Then she coulda left the real stuff at home and only brought the copies with her.'

May gasped. That was the answer and she had been too stupid to see it.

'No, she didn't!' she cried. 'They did!'

They all stared at her. Then she explained about the little box that had been almost empty one night and nearly full the next, although Scruffy had been stitching on jewels all day.

'That's it,' Whacker said excitedly. 'They got copies and Scruffy had to stitch some of them on otherwise it woulda looked funny. But as soon as they nicked the real jewels she took off the copies and stitched the real ones on instead.'

'And that's why she got so behind with her work,' May said, still working it out, 'because she had to do a whole lot of it over again. No wonder she didn't like me lookin' into the box.'

'And she'd have to keep all the fake ones,' Richie said. 'Because the minute she gets to Liverpool, she's gonna have to switch them all around again. Then Nick and Slasher can take the real ones to the fence and flog them and no one will suspect a thing.'

'It's a really good stroke,' Whacker said thoughtfully. 'If the fuzz do search through all the gear goin' on to the boat it's the stuff in the box they'll check, just the way May did.'

'Well?' said Richie, 'What are we gonna do about it?'

They all fell silent at that. Then May spoke slowly; 'We'll go to the fuzz. We'll have to.'

She felt bad about telling on Scruffy. Telling on people was about the worst thing you could do in the Square, but this time there was something worse still. She thought of the show going on for weeks, with Sylvia wearing that emerald at her throat and Slasher hanging about with a knife or a gun maybe.

'Even if they don't believe us at first they'll have to check,' she went on. 'I mean when they're that steamed up over the jewels they couldn't chance ignoring any lead. And once they show the real jewels to someone like Mr. Leventon it'll be proved.'

'No!' cried Maura suddenly. 'You can't!'

Her skin was always pale over her high cheekbones, but now it was white as paper and her green eyes seemed to burn.

'Why not?' asked Whacker.

'You don't even know it's true. You just thought it all up like something you saw on the telly. Yer gonna have the whole theatre pulled apart and maybe find the emerald on the cloak's the very same as this!'

'Maura's right.' Richie said. 'First we gotta make sure. What we gotta do is take the emerald on the cloak to Mr. Leventon.'

'But we can't!' May cried. 'We can't take the cloak outa the Wardrobe. The costumes are always locked up at night.'

'You work there, don't you?' Whacker said. 'You oughta be able to fix it.'

'And then what?' demanded Maura. 'Supposin' yer right and the one on the cloak's the real McCoy, what then?'

'Then we take it to the fuzz,' Whacker said.

Maura turned on him, suddenly raging:

'The fuzz'll come into the theatre askin' everyone questions and rippin' the costumes and maybe take Nick and Scruffy away and the show will be destroyed.'

'They can get someone else in place of them, can't they?'

'No, they can't. You don't understand! You don't work there! You don't know what yer talkin' about!'

Whacker had never seen Maura like this before. Maura, who was usually afraid of her own shadow, had turned on him like some wild animal. He took a step backwards.

May realized then what Maura was on about. She was all keyed up for the first night, thinking only about the show and her part. And what she said was true! If everything was as they suspected it would be almost impossible to have the show good for the opening on Tuesday, the night when the critics came and wrote the show up for the papers and said if they thought it was good or bad.

'It'd take a while for someone else to get the hang of things,' she explained to Whacker. 'It's a terrible bad time to have to replace them.'

Whacker turned then, as he always did in the end, to Richie.

'What d'ye think, Redser?' he asked.

'I dunno,' said Richie, 'but I was thinkin'... maybe if we waited a few days, till after the first night anyway. Then May could watch everything Scruffy did so she would be ready to take over.'

'Wouldn't that be O.K.?' Whacker appealed to Maura.

'Maybe for Scruffy. What about Nick?'

'Maybe you could tell Phil,' May suggested. 'Then she'd be ready to take over from Nick.'

To Whacker's relief, Maura nodded slowly.

'Maybe I could,' she said. 'I'd say she'd believe me all right. And maybe she'd manage if she was expectin' to have to do it. She'd have to have someone to give her a hand, but...'

'So would I,' said May, 'but they'd surely get us both someone.'

'Then that's settled,' Whacker said. 'We do nothing

only keep our eyes open till the show's runnin'. Then May takes the cloak to the pawn. O.K.?'

'Fine!' The colour had come back into Maura's cheeks.

It was amazing, May thought. They all seemed quite happy now, excited even. Only she had a sick feeling in her stomach. It was all right for them. They did not have to steal a cloak out of the Wardrobe or sit day after day beside Scruffy, knowing they were going to betray her. That night she went to bed with the fake emerald hidden under her pillow and dreamed that Scruffy was trying to kill her with Mrs. Mullen's cutting-out scissors.

4 The Pass is Sold

Next morning, May hurried ahead of the others so as to slip the fake emerald back into the box before Scruffy got in, and she had only just done so when she heard Scruffy's feet stumping up the stairs. Was it May's imagination or did her eyes go at once to the press to make sure it was still locked?

'You're in early this morning,' she said, as she took the key from her pocket.

'Yer early yerself,' May retorted.

'I want to get a few things done before the run-through,' Scruffy said, unlocking the cupboard and looking swiftly over the costumes. 'It's supposed to be at ten, though I doubt they'll start on time.'

'Are they doin' the run in costume then?' May asked in surprise.

Scruffy shook her head impatiently.

'That's Monday,' she snapped. 'Don't you ever read what's up on the board?'

May had glanced at the notice board beside the door leading to the stage when waiting for Maura and noticed it had rehearsal times and the scenes to be rehearsed. She realized it must also say when costumes would be worn. She plugged in the iron and began to press Sylvia's cloak.

As she did so the great emerald winked and sparkled and May had a prickly feeling that Scruffy was watching her. She was glad when she had hung the cloak back in the press and started on the chorus boys' tunics that Scruffy had finished stitching the day before.

Mrs. Mullen came in then and, instead of unlocking the drawer where she kept her precious cutting-out scissors, she took a notebook and pencil from a shelf.

'You know we're watching the run-through this morning?' she said.

'I just want to finish off this tunic,' Scruffy said. 'I'll have all done then.'

'Right,' said Mrs. Mullen, 'but May can leave pressing it till this evening. I want the costumes all locked up before we go down.'

'I'll see to it,' Scruffy said. 'You two go on and I'll be straight down after you.'

May unplugged the iron and followed Mrs. Mullen out on to the landing. She had not realized she would be watching the run-through. Instead of finding excuses to slip into the wings to peep at snatches of rehearsal, as she had peeped at Maura's audition on that first day, she

47

would now be able to watch the whole thing openly from start to finish and during her working hours too! She was going to be paid for doing what she most wanted to do. It was a gift.

'Why do we watch the run-through?' she asked.

'So we know the run of the show,' Mrs. Mullen explained. 'We see where the quick changes come and decide which of us will help with what change. In some cases we will have to have the costumes ready in the wings.'

Instead of going through the door that led on to the stage, Mrs. Mullen tapped on the office door. A man's voice called out, 'Come in!' and May followed her into the room with the big office desk and swivel chair.

'Just going through to watch the run-through,' Mrs. Mullen told the manager and she crossed the office and opened a door on the far side. Following her down three steps May found herself in a passage sloping downwards.

'Where are we?' she asked.

'This is the way the audience comes in,' Mrs. Mullen told her. 'Back that way is the box-office and the main entrance in Dame Street. This way takes us into the auditorium. We're below stage level now and the door opposite takes you in under the stage and into the band-room. That's how the orchestra goes through to the pit.'

May had often looked down into the dark, railed-off area between the stage and the front row of seats, where the piano and all the chairs and music-stands were, and wondered how the musicians got into it. She knew they came out of a little door at the back under the stage, but where that led she had not known before. Mrs. Mullen

48

pushed open a swing door and they were in the auditorium.

A little cluster of people were sitting near the front of the otherwise empty theatre in the middle of the front row of the second block of seats. It had a wide passage running in front of it and in this had been placed a table covered in papers, plans and a large notebook. May recognized the woman sitting behind it as the director and the woman beside her the designer.

'Who are the men?' she whispered to Mrs. Mullen, as they slipped into the seats in the same row.

'The big man at the end is the lighting director,' Mrs. Mullen whispered back,' and the man with the grey hair the musical director. He'll be conducting the orchestra for the run-through tomorrow, but it's only piano today.'

May nodded. She remembered now that she had seen him playing the piano at one of the rehearsals.

'And the other two?' she asked.

'I don't know. Maybe the author and the composer. It would be natural enough for them to come to a run-through.'

May looked up at the boxes on either side of the stage, where people could sit in groups on moveable chairs. They had a funny old-fashioned look with their little curtains, and May thought how splendid they would seem when all the lights were on instead of just a few.

A rumbling sound from the stage made May look up in time to see two men push away the cottage that was part of the set for that evening's show. It seemed much lighter than it looked and, from the way it moved, she thought it must be on wheels. Now the huge stage was bare except for the great blue cloth across the back.

'Are we ready to start?' the director called and Nick came out from the wings.

'Two minutes,' he said and disappeared again.

The men who had wheeled off the cottage came in with a couch which they set up a little to one side, and Nick followed with a goat's skin, which he flung over it.

'We're not using that couch, are we?' said the director.

'Oh no, that's only for the rehearsal,' said the designer, 'but I'm thinking of using that goatskin. You can see how it looks with the set on Monday.'

Suddenly the great red curtain fell, hiding the stage. Nick stuck his head out between the folds.

'We're ready now if you are,' he said.

The director nodded and Nick's head disappeared. May heard the seat beside her bang down and saw Scruffy had joined them. Then she heard chords on the piano. The run-through had started.

The curtain rose again and the first thing she saw was Richie. He was in a group at the front of the stage, with Mickser and Imelda in the background, and she heard the designer say:

'Of course the gauze will be between them and the couch.'

May supposed Richie would not look so stupid when he was in the tunic Scruffy had made. Then they started to sing the opening number and she even forgot it was Richie. The music had a great swing to it and each chorus ended with them all singing together: *Maeve, Queen of Connacht.*

After that came the scene with Maeve and Ailill.

They had a song May thought very funny when they were counting how much they each owned and May laughed out loud when Sylvia sang: 'Five hundred chamber-pots' and pulled out a tin po from under the couch.

'I'm going to paint it gold,' the designer said.

Then Maura came on. She stood all on her own, her arms stretched out in front of her as if she was holding something and her voice range out, sweet and true. May felt terribly proud of her. Then suddenly she caught the word 'cloak' as Maura came down to Sylvia and pretended to clasp something about her shoulders, and a little shiver ran through her. She had worried about Sylvia wearing the cloak with the great emerald at her throat, but it was Maura who would be standing holding it every night in the wings, waiting for her entrance; Maura who would be the easiest for Slasher to take it from if he became scared that something had gone wrong. Mrs. Mullen tapped her on the shoulder.

'I'm giving you Sylvia's change after this scene,' she said. 'You'll have to be ready to take the cloak from her and help her into her battle gear.'

May nodded, but her heart gave a bit of a lurch. They were all in it!

'I could do that one,' Scruffy said quickly, but Mrs. Mullen shook her head.

'You'll have to look after Ailill,' she said. 'His change is a really fast one. You'll need to do it in the scene dock.'

May took a quick glance sideways and saw Scruffy was frowning. And she would be left with the cloak, there in the darkened wings. She found it hard to keep her mind on the business of costume changes.

When it came to the battle scenes they were using the real weapons and shields and May realized for the first time that some had a single large stone on each hilt.

As the curtain came down at the close of the first half, the director turned to the two men.

'How are you enjoying it?' she asked.

'Very much!' the first man replied. 'When it's tightened up a bit and you have costumes, lights and orchestra, I think it should work very well.'

'Yes, indeed,' said the second man. 'And the weapons are great. They look just like the real thing.'

'You can thank Nick for that,' the designer replied. 'He knew someone who made them for a film in Ardmore.'

May felt a shiver down her spine and she watched the second half in a daze. Maura's big moment was over but the other three were in and out of the action for the big numbers, particularly the one which told of the fight between the two bulls. It was an exciting story and ordinarily May would have been totally gripped by it, but now she found herself all the time watching Cúchulainn's sword or Conor's little ceremonial dagger or the great shield with which Fergus protected Maeve.

At the end of the run-through, crossing the office with Mrs. Mullen and Scruffy, she hesitated.

'May I go and see Maura, just for a second,' she begged.

'All right, but don't be long,' Mrs. Mullen told her. 'We need everything for the dress rehearsal.'

On her way to the stage, May noticed the doorman talking to someone. He was a heavily built man with unusually long arms and a scar running down his left cheek. There was no mistaking him from her brother's description. Slasher was mounting guard over his property.

He glanced up and May saw the look on his face. If ever she tried to take the cloak out of the theatre to show it to Mr. Leventon, as Richie had planned, he would be there waiting for her. Trembling, she hurried on to the stage, where the cast were all grouped around the director.

'Well done, Maura,' May heard her say, before the group broke up and Maura joined her in the wings.

'You were only great,' May enthused, trying to hide the shake in her voice. Usually Maura was quick to notice if anyone was upset about anything but now her mind was only on the show.

'Are you comin' home for yer dinner?' she asked.

'I can't. I've still things to do and I gotta see Richie.'

'You'd better hurry,' Maura said. 'We've to run over some of the battle scenes again.'

'Will you tell Mammy I'll get something across the road?' May called after her, and grabbed Richie's arm as the director gave a last note to the actor who played Cúchulainn. Richie went with her into the scene dock.

'We'll have to forget about gettin' proof,' she whispered, and told him about Slasher.

Richie looked serious.

'I know we promised Maura,' he said, 'but I don't think we're gonna be able to wait till after the first night.'

Suddenly May felt her shoulders gripped from behind and saw Richie's eyes widen. Turning, she found the hands which held her fast were Nick's.

'Betty warned me you'd been sniffing around the Wardrobe,' he said, 'so I've been keeping an eye on you and your pals. I think it's time we had a little talk.'

'I'm not finished on stage yet,' Richie protested, but Nick ignored him.

'This way, ' he said pushing them up the ladder-like steps to the fly-rail.

Neither of them had been up there before and they looked around them in amazement while they recovered their breath, for it was a steep climb up. The narrow cat-walk high above the stage ran around three sides, facing the proscenium arch into the auditorium. Here were the ropes that hauled the scenery up and down and the batteries of flood-lights and spotlights set so that they would shine down on the actors below.

'It's a long way down,' Nick said. 'Anyone falling from here would most likely be killed.'

They stepped back from him fast, clinging to the handrail and he smiled nastily.

'I'm glad you get the message,' he said, 'but I wasn't thinking of giving you a push... for the moment. But you see those big heavy floods? If one of them fell I wouldn't hold out much hope for anyone standing right underneath. And I'd say your young friend who plays the servant stands pretty well directly under that one over there for her first entrance, wouldn't you?'

May felt a prickling sensation at the back of her neck and when she spoke her voice came out in a sort of a squeak.

'What are you saying?' she croaked.

Nick smiled again, but it was not a nice smile.

'Just this: I don't know what you know, or think you

54

know, but keep it to yourselves if you don't want there to be a terrible accident. If you or that other pair breathe one word to anyone you needn't come crying to me if one of these floods should accidentally crash to the stage at an unfortunate moment. D'you get me?'

'Loud and clear,' said Richie. 'And now please get outa my way. They're waitin' on me.'

With a mock bow Nick stood aside, and feeling as if she was choking, May followed Richie back down the steps to the stage. There was absolutely nothing they would dare to do now. They would have to watch the jewels being shipped to Liverpool in helpless silence.

5   Three Brass Balls

In the end, Maura was the only one to get home for her dinner. The others barely had time for a quick cup of tea in the snack-bar in Dame Street before May had to be back in Wardrobe and rehearsals began again.

'It's gone two o'clock,' Imelda's mother said to Whacker. 'D'you think is she all right?'

'Of course she's all right, ' he said. 'They musta been kept late, that's all.'

'She'll be starved with the hunger,' his mother said. 'Would you ever run down with a sandwich for her?'

So, vainly protesting, Whacker set off for the Olympia with sandwiches in a plastic bag. As he crossed the Square, Patchie bounded up to him, glad to see at least one member of the gang. He and Patchie were both fed up with rock musicals, Whacker thought. They might as well join forces. He set off down Capel Street with Patchie at his heels.

This time the stage doorman would not let him in.

'She's rehearsing,' he said, when Whacker demanded to see his sister. 'You can't see her now.'

'I've brought her lunch,' Whacker said.

'Bit late in the day, aren't you?' the stage doorman said. 'You'd better leave it with me and I'll give it to her when she's finished.'

'But it'll be tea-time by then!' Whacker protested.

'Can't help that,' the man said. 'Leave it or not as you like, but you can't stand here,' and he went to push Whacker out of the doorway.

But he had reckoned without Patchie, who decided to defend his master's pal and hurled himself at the man, growling viciously. The doorman sprang back, but not before the bundle of white fur had set his teeth firmly in the leg of his trousers.

'Hey!' yelled the doorman. 'Get that little divil off me!' And he shook his leg backwards and forwards, while Patchie clung on obstinately.

A woman ran out of the office to see what the shouting was about, and a heavily built man with a scar on his cheek, who had been lounging about in the lane, sauntered over towards them. Whacker decided it was time to go. While all attention was on Patchie he slipped in through the door that led to the stage.

Imelda was not there — only a tall actor arguing with someone out amongst the seat rows. Then Whacker spotted her in the middle of a group of people on the far side of the stage.

To avoid crossing it, he retraced his steps, popping

56

round behind the cloth. Suddenly in the dim light he saw a gaping hole in front of him and only stopped just in time to avoid plunging into it. The lid of a trapdoor was lifted and he could see steps leading down. Picking his way cautiously around it, he joined the group.

Imelda, talking to Richie and Mickser in whispers, looked up in surprise as Whacker came over to her.

'I brought you a sandwich,' he said.

'Great!' said Mickser. 'I'm famished. Give us a bite, Melly?'

There were three sandwiches and she gave one each to Richie and Mickser. They were gone in a flash.

'Yous weren't long milling them!' Whacker said admiringly.

'We're on!' said Imelda suddenly, and the three of them were gone.

Whacker looked around him. There was no one left in the wings. They were all on stage, marching and shouting. The tall actor who had been arguing suddenly ran by him, throwing something down on a table as he passed. It was, Whacker saw, a dagger, and a large red stone glinted on the handle. Whacker did not stop to think. He slipped it into his pocket and ran out through the scene dock door.

The little glass sentry-box was deserted and there was no sign of stage doorman, woman or Patchie, so he slipped quickly out into the lane. There was no one there either, except for the man with a scar on his face, who watched Whacker with interest as he ran down the lane towards East Essex Street.

On stage, the scene where the Connacht court jester goes to the Ulster camp disguised as Ailill was interrupted by the sound of angry voices in the scene dock.

'I tell you, I left it back on the prop table,' Roger could be heard shouting.

'Well then, where is it?' came Nick's reply.

Jane sighed and halted the action. 'Ask Jimmy to come here for a moment, will you?' she called.

Nick strode on stage, his face like thunder.

'What seems to be the trouble now?' Jane asked.

'There are too many amateurs in the cast of this show, that's the trouble,' he spat out.

'This show is supposed to open on Tuesday,' Jane pointed out coldly, 'though if we keep having these interruptions I don't know! What exactly happened?'

'It took a great deal of time, trouble and expense to make these props,' Nick said, 'and they can't be replaced overnight. I keep them locked in the prop cupboard when they're not in use; I won't be responsible if they're not put back on the prop table.'

'That's hardly sufficient reason to interrupt my rehearsal,' said Jane, 'but since we're stopped will everyone please note that no props other than personal props are to be taken to the dressing-rooms for any reason whatsoever.'

'What's a personal prop?' Maura whispered to Phil.

'Something you have with you right through the show, like a fan or a cane,' Phil told her. 'A sword could be a personal prop, but Cúchulainn's isn't because George brings it on and buckles it on him on stage.'

'But I *didn't* take my dagger to the dressing-room,' shouted Roger, who had followed Nick back on stage. 'I put it back on the prop table.'

'Then someone took it off again,' stormed Nick.

'Are you sure it hasn't fallen down behind the table?' Jane asked wearily.

'Quite sure,' Nick said, giving Richie a nasty look, 'And if one of the kids in the chorus took it I won't be responsible for what happens.'

'Did any of you see Ailill's dagger since Roger's last exit?' Jane asked, addressing the whole cast.

They all shook their heads.

'Well,' she said, 'if it's not found soon we'll have to organize a proper search. Now, please, can we go back to just before Ailill's exit?'

Phil turned back a page in her big prompt book.

'Take it from Maeve's line: "This is a crime, this slaughter of our people,"' she said.

Everyone regrouped and Roger took up his place once more. Nick, with a last unpleasant look at Richie, withdrew into the wings.

Again Ailill outlined his plan to trick Cúchulainn, and again his crown was placed on the jester's head and his cloak around his shoulders. Again Ailill refused to give his dagger also, telling the jester to stand at a little distance from Cúchulainn so neither he nor his dagger could be too clearly seen.

But when he said: 'Take the girl with you, and pretend to betroth her to Cúchulainn,' and Richie led Imelda, at that point playing the small non-speaking part of Finnabair, down stage, there was a sudden cry of 'Look out!' and Imelda staggered forward, her hand to her head. Everyone crowded around her.

'Are you all right?' cried Jane, climbing up on to the stage.

'I think so,' Imelda said, dazed. A small trickle of blood was running down the side of her face.

'It's only a surface cut,' said Phil. 'Keep your dirty fingers away from it.'

'Run up to the Wardrobe,' Jane said. 'There's a first-aid box there. Mrs. Mullen will bathe it for you, and put a drop of disinfectant in the water. What fell?'

'It's only a gel,' said Nick, coming back on stage. 'One of the lads must have dropped it off the fly-rail.'

Then Maura saw a piece of blue shiny stuff in a metal frame, like the ones she had noticed on the front of the powerful flood-lamps above.

'Well, please tell them to be more careful in future,' Jane said, as Richie led Imelda off stage. 'I don't want to lose any of my cast!'

'Indeed,' said Nick, looking straight at Richie as he passed. 'Supposing it had been the flood itself and not just the gel!'

When Richie brought Imelda into the Wardrobe and told them what had happened, May went white. She slipped out after Richie, who was hurrying back to rehearsal.

'For pity's sake, put the dagger back,' she whispered, 'before one of us is killed!'

Richie stared at his sister in amazement.

'You don't imagine I lifted it after what Nick said, do you?' he asked indignantly. 'I'm not that crazy!'

'Then who did? Mickser? Or Melly herself?'

'No way!' said Richie. 'They were both on stage with me from Roger's exit until Nick blew up. I was thinkin' it musta been you, only I couldn't believe it.'

'Could it have been Maura?'

Richie shook his head: 'She was on the prompt side with Phil. I dunno what happened it, but it wasn't any of us.'

'But Nick thinks we did,' said May. 'And if he doesn't get it back soon he'll drop that flood on Maura like he said he would. We gotta find it!'

Suddenly Richie gasped. 'Whacker!' he said.

'What?'

'Whacker lifted it. He musta done! And he didn't know Nick had warned us off!'

'But how could Whacker have taken it? He wasn't here!'

'He was,' Richie said. 'He was down with sandwiches for Imelda. And he was standin' right by the prop table when we went back stage!'

'Then that's it!' May cried, white-faced. 'Somebody's gotta go after him and get it back!'

'How?' asked Richie. 'I gotta get back to rehearsal, and Jane wants Melly back the minute she feels O.K. Can you find some excuse to slip out?'

May shook her head:

'I've a pile of pressing to do. There's a panic on with the dress rehearsal Monday. There's no way Mrs. Mullen would give me half an hour off now.'

As if to underline her words, Imelda came out of the Wardrobe, a piece of sticking-plaster on her forehead.

'You'd better go back in, May!' she said. 'Mrs. Mullen's givin' out yards about you.'

'What are we gonna do?' May asked Richie, frantic.

'I'll think of something,' said Richie, and he and Imelda hurried off down the stairs.

May went back to her ironing, but her mind was not

on her work. All the time she was seeing Maura lying unconscious on the stage, the heavy flood, with its lens shattered, beside her head. And she kept on wondering how on earth they were going to get back Ailill's dagger?

Whacker was just beginning to wonder the very same thing. At Leventons in Capel Street, the man in the pawn had looked at him with narrowed eyes.

'And how, may I ask, did you come by the likes of this?' he had enquired suspiciously.

Maybe Mr. Leventon might have believed Whacker's yarn, but his assistant obviously did not and Whacker became afraid he would ring the gardaí.

'I'm not not trying to sell it or pawn it,' he pointed out. 'Only to find out what it's worth.'

'We charge for valuations,' the man told him, 'but I can tell you this! It's worth enough for anyone that owns it to take better care of it than to let a young lad carry it around loose in his pocket.'

'I'll tell that to the boss,' said Whacker, edging towards the door.

'Hang on a minute,' the man began, but Whacker was in the street and mingling with the crowds outside the bookies before the man had cleared the counter. Only when Whacker was sure he was not being followed did he start to wonder how he would get the dagger back again, without Patchie to help him now. He would have to wait and give it to the others that evening to take back with them next day. There was no point in going to the Olympia now, so he turned towards St. Mary's Abbey.

At that moment, he heard a shout and saw Maura racing up Capel Street from the bridge.

'Did you take Ailill's dagger offa the prop table in the

theatre?' she gasped, as she came up with him.

'Yeah,' said Whacker. 'Was it missed?'

'Hasn't the whole place gone mad lookin' for it?' she said. 'For pity's sake, give it me quick!'

She had a carrier-bag with her and Whacker slid the dagger quickly from his pocket and into the bag. Maura breathed a sigh of relief.

'You near had us all killed,' she said. 'We gotta give up the idea of takin' the jewels to the pawn. It's too dangerous.'

'Already done,' said Whacker smugly. 'And I was right, what's more! That ruby's the real McCoy.'

Maura looked at him for a moment and Whacker saw real fear in her eyes. Then she gave a little shiver, turned on her heels and fled back the way she had come.

At the Olympia the rehearsal was coming to an end.

'That's it,' said Jane finally, 'except for the curtain calls. Can I have everyone on stage, please?'

They all assembled and Jane lined them up in a half-circle facing the audience, with Sylvia in the middle and the chorus grouped in the corners.

'That's your final position,' she said. 'Now I have to work out how I'm going to get you there.' Then suddenly she paused: 'Wait a minute! Someone's missing! Where's Maura?'

Phil came out from the prompt corner saying: 'She can't be far away. She was beside me at the start of the last scene.'

Richie, looking rather uneasy, said: 'Maybe she thought we were finished.'

'She knows perfectly well she can't go until I say so,' Jane said, and shouted for Nick.

'Did you say that Maura could go?' she asked him.

'I certainly did not,' he answered.

'Well, she seems to have disappeared,' Jane said.

'Like Ailill's dagger,' Nick said darkly. 'Odd, isn't it, how they both disappeared from the same rehearsal?'

'Are you suggesting that Maura had something to do with the disappearance of the dagger?' Jane enquired.

'I'm only saying it's odd,' Nick said. 'And I don't want anyone leaving this theatre till that dagger is found.'

At that moment, Maura walked on to the stage, the dagger in her hand.

'Here's your old dagger,' she said, holding it out to Nick. 'I thought since I wasn't in the last act I'd have a hunt for it. It was down behind the corner of one of the flats in the scene dock. It musta got knocked offa the prop table and kicked in behind the flat.'

'Good on you, Maura,' said Jane. 'Well, that's one storm in a teacup over anyway!'

But Nick muttered: 'Funny coincidence all the same!' and Rickie knew that they would be watched even more closely now.

6   A Stranger Calls

That Sunday was the longest day Maura ever remembered. It seemed to go on and on for ever, yet tired though she was, she could not rest. In only two days time she would have to walk out on to the stage knowing that hundreds of pairs of eyes were on her as she sang.

64

Her mother and father were no help at all.

'I dunno what yer complainin' about,' her father said. 'Aren't you gettin' paid for it? I only wish I had a job the like of it. It's money for jam!'

'And you was the one wanted to do it,' her mother added. 'The dear knows you oughta know what it is yer at by now. You've been practisin' long enough!'

But Maura knew that no matter how many times she rehearsed, nothing would be the same when it was not just Jane out there in the darkness, but people who had paid to see the show and, worse still, people who would be writing about it in the papers afterwards.

She washed her red-gold hair till it was as shiny as the chestnuts they had collected for conkers. Then she set out on her bike for the North Circular Road to tell Linda and her grandfather there were two tickets at the box-office for them for Tuesday night. Linda would not be able to see the lovely costumes, but she would be able to hear Maura sing.

May found an excuse to run over to the theatre. She wanted to see the cloths for the previous show being taken down off the lines that lifted them into the flies, and their own lovely cloths tied on in place of them. She crouched in the darkness as they raised the great cloth of gauze and lit it from the spotlights in front so that all you could see was the royal standard of Connacht unfurled across it. Then, at a signal from the lighting director, the front spotlights went out and the great floods that hung centre stage came up so that you could see through the gauze to the royal bedchamber beyond. Then Nick cued the man on the flies and the gauze slowly rose and disappeared.

65

It was like magic, May thought, wishing for a moment she could be out in the audience watching it all.

Imelda spent the evening putting cold compresses on the big black bruises that had come up around the cut on her forehead. It looked awful and not at all right for Finnabair, the intended bride of Cúchulainn, but her mother said it would probably have gone by Tuesday night and anyway couldn't she cover it with make-up?

The three boys hung around the Square, wondering what they should do now in the light of Nick's threats. Mickser was all for taking action then and there.

'Today's the one day Nick can't be watchin' us,' he pointed out. 'The fuz could search the theatre now! We're none of us there for him to do anything to us!'

Whacker knew he was right. They had the proof they needed now and what happened to the show didn't matter to him. It mattered to Maura though. He remembered the way she had gone white when they first suggested calling in the guards and the fear in her green eyes yesterday when he told her the ruby was real.

'Don't you care what happens the show?' he asked.

'There's a big reward offered for them jewels!' Mickser retorted, 'And I'm only in the chorus.'

'That goes for the rest of us too,' said Richie, 'But we promised Maura and a promise is a promise, isn't that right, Whacker?'

'That's right, Redser,' said Whacker loyally.

'That's two to one then,' Richie said.

'It's not fair,' Mickser complained sullenly. 'Whacker always backs you!'

'Then we'll get the girls and vote again,' Richie said. 'Don't you know well May and Maura will vote with you two,' Mickser snorted. 'It'd be only Melly and me against yous.'

'And I wouldn't be too sure about Melly either,' said Whacker, for his sister had surprised him in the past few days. She had begun, like Mickser, by being interested only in the money and the crack, but since they had begun rehearsing in the theatre itself she had started talking for all the world like May and Maura.

'Right!' said Richie. 'That's settled then. Let's get the bikes and go for a spin.'

Maura had not meant Linda's grandfather to find out about the jewels. It was not their habit in the Square to involve outsiders and she knew Richie and May would not want him told. But she just had to tell Linda and, before Maura could stop her, Linda had blurted the whole thing out to him. The old man was horrified.

'You must go to the gardaí at once,' he said.

'We can't till the show's running,' Maura told him.

'But as long as you delay you could be in danger,' the old man protested. 'Maybe that stage manager fellow is only bluffing about what he'd do to you, but the man hanging around outside the stage door sounds capable of anything!'

'If Nick and Scruffy were arrested now the show would be wrecked,' Maura said, and she explained how Phil had agreed to understudy Nick and May was getting ready to take over from Scruffy.

'I'm afraid those two aren't all that would need replacing,' Linda's grandfather said. 'Don't you realize the gardaí will take possession of all the costumes and weapons with jewels on them?'

Maura went white in the face.

'Then we can't tell the cops at all,' she said flatly.

'I'm afraid, my dear, you must,' the old man replied. 'Your lives are more important than the show.'

But if anything went wrong with the show now her life wouldn't be worth living, Maura thought in despair.

'Did you say Scruffy had kept the fake jewels to put back on again when the show got to Liverpool?' Linda asked suddenly.

Maura nodded. But what did all that matter now?

'Well then,' said Linda triumphantly, 'Why can't May swap them around again now? Then you can take the real ones to the police.'

For a second Maura brightened. Then she became gloomy again.

'It would take ages for her to change them back again,' she said. 'Besides, the cops would never believe we hadn't nicked the jewels ourselves if we just took them back.'

'They'd believe grand-dad,' Linda said. 'You could give them to him to hand over.'

'Would you really do that?' Maura asked the old man.

'Of course I would,' he told her. 'I haven't forgotten how you and your friends saved my life. How soon could you give them to me?'

'The minute the first night is over, if May can manage it,' Maura said.

'We can get them from you when we come to the show on Tuesday,' Linda said. 'We'll come round to the stage door afterwards.'

'Oh no, you won't,' her grandfather said. 'It might be

dangerous. I'll go round on my own. But Maura must promise if things get dangerous in the meantime she won't wait till then.'

'All right, I promise,' said Maura, but she crossed her fingers behind her back as she said it. It was only forty-eight hours until the first night. They would hang on somehow. Then a dreadful thought struck her.

'But what about the jewels on the swords and daggers?' she asked. 'There's no way we'd be able to get them.'

'Leave them where they are,' Linda's grandfather said. 'It will help to prove your story. I know a director of the Abbey Theatre and I'm sure he'll be able to arrange for you to borrow all you need from them until you can get new stuff. They should have plenty of suitable weapons with all the Yeats plays they've done.'

When she got back to the Square, Maura went straight to May's house and Richie called a meeting of the gang, asking each in turn what they thought of Linda's plan.

'I like it,' Mickser said at once. 'It's definite about who does what and it wastes no time. So long as Linda's grand-dad isn't lookin' for a share in the reward.'

May turned on him angrily: 'Of course he's not. But how d'ye think I can sew on all them fake jewels before Tuesday night?'

'We could all give you a hand,' offered Imelda.

'Not Maura!' May said quickly. 'Don't you know if she's tired it'll show in her voice? And the boys would only be a hindrance.'

'May's right,' said Richie. 'The whole plan depends on her so it's for her to decide.'

'When would I get to do it?' asked May. 'It took Scruffy most of the night to sew them on in the first place.'

'And that's the very way you'll have to change them back,' Whacker told her. 'If you had Melly to help you, could you do them in a night?'

'Oh, sure,' May nodded, 'Only I've no key to the press. There's no way I could get at the costumes once that's locked up. Mrs. Mullen's insisting on keeping them all there to make sure they're clean and pressed.'

'That's where we come in,' said Whacker, 'If you can get the key out to me some way durin' the rehearsal, I'll get a copy made,'

'But Nick musta smuggled Scruffy back into the theatre the night she did them,' May protested. 'How are Melly and me to get into the Wardrobe at night?'

'You'll only have to hide when everyone else is leavin',' Richie said. 'We'll say yous have already gone on. Just tell me this and tell me no more; if we can get you a key to the press and you manage to stay in the theatre overnight, will you do it?'

'I will,' May said, 'if Melly will really stay with me. I'd be scared to be in the place all night be meself. The theatre's haunted, you know.'

'Didn't I already say I'd stay?' said Imelda. 'And anyways I never seen any signs of a ghost.'

So next morning, telling her mother she would be staying the night with Mrs. Mullen because she might have to work till all hours, May set off for the theatre.

'I want all the costumes laid out ready, with the name of the wearer on them,' Mrs. Mullen told her. 'Jane wants to see all of them on the set before the dress rehearsal and the whole cast will likely descend on us at the one time.'

'There's not much room,' said May, looking from the costumes hanging in the press to the table.

'Only put out the Act One costumes,' Mrs. Mullen said, 'And if anyone has a change during Act One, leave their second costume on the hanger. But make sure you have them separated from the Act Two costumes.'

'I'll put those down the far end of the press,' May said.

'Betty and I will look after the principals,' Mrs. Mullen continued, 'and you can see to the chorus.'

May thought Mrs. Mullen was making an awful fuss about nothing for by now they all knew who was wearing what, but when the cast arrived and started milling around she realized Mrs. Mullen had been wise.

'Those aren't yours, Mickser,' she said hastily, snatching a pile of clothes from him as he was about to take them out of the room. 'Yours are on the radiator.'

But, in the end, all was sorted out.

'I'm going down to sit with Jane and take a note of anything she's not happy about,' Mrs. Mullen said then. 'You two stay here to hand out the next lot and cope with any problem.' And she was gone, leaving May alone with Scruffy.

It was the first time May had been alone with Scruffy since they had had the show-down with Nick, and she glanced nervously at her. If only she would go out of the room for a minute May could slip the key of the press into the pocket of her jeans ready to pass it on to the boys as soon as she got the chance. But Scruffy showed no signs of going anywhere. Instead, she took out a magazine from her pocket and began to read.

May had not thought of bringing anything to read, so she looked around for something to do. She decided to tidy the box with all the sewing threads in it, but all the time she worked she felt Scruffy was watching her to see if she would go near the little box that held the false jewels.

Maura, too, had time to kill. She had only one costume and Jane had not been long in passing it. Maura had hardly moved down into the pool of light and turned slowly around when Jane called out:

'That's fine. Next!'

Another problem worried Maura. She had never used make-up before, let alone for the stage, so she had asked Phil's advice. 'It's only a straight juv. job,' Phil had told her. 'Just a darker foundation and a bit more colour than normal and lots of eye make-eye. I'll get you a few bits and pieces.' And she had also shown Maura how to enlarge her eyes by extending them at the outer edges and to put tiny red dots in the inner corners to correct the balance.

'Now I must go,' she had said. 'I've a million and one things to do. Just remember to blend the foundation well down on to your neck and throat. Otherwise there'll be a line where it ends and you'll look as if you're wearing a mask.'

'Thanks, Phil. You're a real star!' Maura had said gratefully. She would have hated to have had to ask Jane or Sylvia about make-up and everyone seemed to have taken it for granted that she knew all about things like that. Now there was nothing left to do but to sit and wait.

Waiting gave her too much time to think, too much time to worry. Suppose May got caught switching the jewels around? She could feel the muscles in her throat tightening with nerves.

Suddenly there was a knock on the door and, before she could even say 'Come in!' it opened. In the mirror facing her she saw Nick, standing in the open doorway. She spun around on the stool, stifling a scream.

Nick grinned, closed the door behind him and locked it. Then he put the key in his pocket.

'Just to make sure we're not interrupted,' he told her.

'What d'ye want?' Maura gasped.

'The answers to a few questions for a start,' he said. 'Where did you really get Ailill's dagger?'

'I told you,' Maura stammered. 'Down behind the flat in the scene dock.'

'Don't waste my time,' Nick said angrily. 'You were seen leaving the stage door and you only came back just before you appeared on stage.'

'Who says so?' Maura asked desperately.

'Someone very interested in that dagger,' said Nick,

Maura thought again about the tall man with the scar on his face who was always out in the lane.

'He wouldn't be too fussy about what happened to anyone that got in his way,' Nick said. 'So if you don't want to get hurt better tell me the truth.'

'There's nothing to tell,' Maura said lamely, Her mind was racing. Where could she say she had been?

'Who d'you think you're codding?' Nick demanded. 'It was you took the dagger off the prop table in the first place, wasn't it?'

'I wasn't near yer oul' prop table,' Maura shouted

indignantly. That at least was true. 'I was in the prompt corner from the end of my scene until you said the dagger was missing. Ask Phil if you don't believe me!'

'So why did you leave the theatre?'

'That's my business!'

'Ah, now that's just where you're wrong, my lady. You're not allowed to leave the theatre without permission and well you know it!'

'Jane was busy. I didn't want to be botherin' her when I was only goin' for five minutes.'

'You could have asked me.'

What was she going to say? Suddenly she remembered the crash that had made her nearly jump out of her skin as she ran for the stage door. It was a gift.

'You were busy too at the time,' she said. 'You were cueing the thunderclaps.'

She had a plausible answer for everything, Nick thought.

'You still haven't said where you went.'

'It's personal,' Maura said. 'I'd to get to a chemist urgent-like.'

She knew from the baffled look on Nick's face that her sudden inspiration had been a good one. It would be a difficult lie to nail down. At that moment, she heard the welcome voice of Phil coming over the dressing-room Tannoy.

'Quarter of an hour to dress rehearsal,' she said. 'Quarter of an hour, please! And Jimmy Clarke's wanted at the stage door!'

With a look of irritation, Nick took the key from his pocket and unlocked the dressing-room door.

'You all think you're very clever,' he said, 'But you'll

find you've bitten off more than you can chew if you try to take me on!'

He opened the door and went out into the passage. Maura rose, trembling. She made a resolution to keep the dressing-room door key in her own pocket in future.

Then Nick turned back for a parting shot:

'Just tell your friends they'd better give me no more trouble if they want to see you safe and well!'

He went down to the stage door to find Slasher standing there.

'This man's asking for you,' the stage doorman said.

'I can't talk to you now,' Nick told Slasher. 'I've a dress rehearsal in a quarter of an hour.'

'I just thought you might like to know,' Slasher said ominously, 'that two of the lads in the chorus brought a pal in with them, saying he'd permission to watch the rehearsal.'

'Which two lads?' asked Nick, suddenly interested.

'The redhead out of the chorus and his pal with glasses,' the doorman said. 'He had permission all right though.'

'I'll keep my eyes open,' Nick promised. 'That pair need watching.'

'So does their pal,' the doorman chipped in. 'The little divil set his dog on me yesterday. My leg was cut right through my trousers. Had to go up to Wardrobe for the first-aid box and put plaster on it.'

'What happened to the lad?' asked Nick. Things were beginning to add up.

'By the time I'd beaten the mongrel off me he'd vanished,' the man said.

At the same time as Ailill's dagger vanished, Nick

thought, but he kept that to himself. If Slasher found out about that there would really be trouble.

At that moment, Whacker came down the stairs from the dressing-rooms, the key of the press in his pocket. May had managed to grab it while Scruffy was giving Roger and Sylvia their quick-change costumes and slipped it to Richie, who had given it to him. The plan had been for him to go through the office with his permission to watch the rehearsal from the stalls and then out by the front entrance as soon as the box-office opened at ten-thirty. Glancing at the clock he saw that it was almost ten-thirty now.

He turned at the foot of the stairs, saw Slasher and Nick at the stage door and knew by the look on their faces that it was no time for bluffing. He dived through the door to the stage, with Nick after him. Plunging behind the back-cloth he suddenly remembererd the trapdoor he had nearly fallen down the day before. In a flash, he had raised it by the metal rings and, crouching on the second step, pulled the lid back into place behind him. He heard the scene dock door swing shut behind Nick and the sound of his footsteps pounding overhead. With his heart pounding almost as loudly, he huddled in the darkness and waited.

7 A Yellow-Eyed Ghost.

How long, Whacker wondered, would he have to wait? He could not see if the coast was clear without raising the lid of the trap, and he had a nightmare vision of himself climbing straight out into Nick's arms. Even if he managed to give Nick the slip, Slasher might still be standing by the open stage door. He wondered where the steps led? It seemed unlikely there was any way out into the lane from under the stage, but it was worth a try.

He groped his way down, and turned to his right. As his eyes grew accustomed to the dark, he saw he was in a small, dusty room with a few chairs and music-stands piled in one corner. There was another door on the far side and, opening it, he found himself in the orchestra pit. Then he heard an all-too-familiar voice coming from right above him.

'Hello, Jane! Are you out there?' the voice said, and Whacker knew Nick must be standing on the edge of the stage, peering out into the darkness of the theatre.

In terror that he might look down, Whacker crept hastily back the way he had come. Suddenly he heard voices ahead of him, the bulb over his head snapped on and light flooded the shabby room. He looked around in vain for somewhere to hide, but already a crowd of people was coming towards him from beyond the steps, talking and laughing. Where from, Whacker did not know, but if they had come in he could go out. He pushed his way past. No one looked at him, obviously thinking he was one of the staff. Opening the door they had just closed he found himself in a well-lit passage.

'Have you any seats left for tomorrow night?' he heard a woman's voice enquire.

To his right he could see daylight and realized he must have ended up exactly where he had originally planned to be; in the passage leading to the auditorium on the far side of the office.

Obviously the box-office was open, and the glass doors leading out into Dame Street would be open too. As he reached the foyer, he saw the front-of-house doorman standing by the door. The man looked at him without suspicion. Ready to stop any intruder from pushing on past the box-office into the theatre, he had no worries about anyone trying to go the other way.

'Good morning,' Whacker said to him politely, and the doorman agreed it was a grand day, as he stood aside for him to pass. Whacker decided to make the most of his opportunity. After all, he had to get both keys back to May, and Slasher might still be guarding the stage door.

'Won't be more than half an hour if anyone's looking for me,' he said, as he strode out into the sunlight.

Back in the theatre the dress rehearsal was finally about to begin. May went carefully through the check list pinned to the wall to make sure she knew everything she had to do up to the interval. They would be breaking for dinner before the second half and she would be able to check the list again then. She collected Sylvia's armour and went down on stage. There she found Maura, standing white-faced in the wings, as the orchestra struck up the overture.

'You'll be all right,' she told her, but Maura only whispered: 'Watch out for Nick. He's been askin' all sorts of questions.'

'What sort of questions?' May asked, but before Maura could answer, Nick appeared.

'You can't stand there,' he said. 'You'll be in the way. Stand over by the door till it's time for your entrance. And *you've* no business here at all!' he said to May.

'I've to be here for Sylvia's quick change,' May told him.

'She's not even on yet,' he snapped. 'I can't have you cluttering up the wings when they're bringing on all the pots and pans. Come down when you see Maura come off.'

Unable to watch from the wings as she had intended, May had to be content to listen but, having seen the run-through, she could picture what was happening, moment by moment, as she stood against the back wall.

Then, all of a sudden, the ground seemed to open up right beside her. She gasped as Whacker's curly head emerged suddenly from the big black hole under the raised trapdoor.

'Psst!' Whacker hissed at her, and with his right arm still holding up the trap he held the left one out to her. On the palm were two identical keys. May took them quickly and slipped them into the pocket of her jeans. Turning back to Whacker, she found nothing but bare boards. He had lowered the trap as silently as he had raised it and departed. She supposed he would now go out front and watch the rehearsal as arranged.

She heard Maura's voice coming from the other side of the back cloth. Was it imagination or had it lost the confident ring it had had at the run-through?

Then Maura was off and she took up her place to wait for Sylvia's exit. When it came, Sylvia flung the cloak at her so that it wrapped itself around her legs. A loose end of thread caught in the zip of the tunic and May struggled to free it while Sylvia swore at her under her breath. Then she was back on stage.

Shaken, May took the cloak and robe back upstairs.

There was no one in the Wardrobe and, with a sigh of relief, she put one of the keys back into the lock of the press. She hoped no one had missed it. It seemed an age since she had stolen it but less than an hour had passed, an hour when everyone's mind had been on the rehearsal. With the duplicate key still burning a hole in her pocket, she set off for No. 4 dressing-room to help Cúchulainn, Fergus and Conor with their armour.

In the end, leaving the girls behind proved easier than they had expected. Whacker had suggested hiding on the stairs under the trap but it was propped open after the rehearsal so the electricians could get up and down from the Electrical Supply Room under the stage. Hiding in the toilet, May had been afraid the doorman would open it, but he only checked the dressing-rooms in a casual way, banging on the doors and trying the handles to see if they were locked.

'Are they all gone from the girls' dressing-rooms?' he asked. 'I didn't notice them leaving.'

'Probably gone out the front way,' Richie said casually. 'I know some of them wanted to book.'

May watched from the Wardrobe window as he set off down the lane. There was no sign of Slasher. With the duplicate key she unlocked the press, and lifted down the little box that held the fake jewels.

'We gotta make sure they look exactly the same afterwards,' she told Imelda, 'Or Scruffy will notice. We've to match each one up and stitch it on the very same as the ones that are on now.'

They worked methodically for an hour or so. At first they talked in whispers about the rehearsal, about what Nick had said to Maura and about how Whacker had found his way through the trapdoor, but soon they became too tired to chat. Twice Imelda found herself beginning to nod.

'Janey!' she said. 'I wish we had a sup of tea!'

'So do I,' May said. 'I'm awful tired. Are you?'

'I could sleep standin' up,' Imelda told her.

Suddenly there was a crash outside and then a distant padding sound. They froze with horror.

'It must be the ghost!' gasped May.

The sound seemed to be coming towards them, for it got louder.

'It's comin' from the dressing-room down the passage!' Imelda whispered.

'I know,' May whispered back. 'And that's the one that's supposed to be haunted!' She looked at Imelda in horror. 'Oh, Melly,' she breathed, 'I'm scared!'

Suddenly Imelda stood lup and strode to the door.

'Don't open it!' May cried, but Imelda took no notice. She flung the door wide and then let out a scream as a pair of yellow eyes stared at her out of the darkness.

The cat, as frightened as Imelda herself, gave a screech and fled for the stairs. The girls collapsed in hysterical laughter.

'There's yer ghost,' giggled Imelda. 'She musta got in through a window.'

'She lives here,' May gasped, dabbing her eyes, for she had laughed until she was crying. 'She's the theatre cat !'

'Oh well,' Imelda said. 'At least that woke me up. I don't feel at all sleepy now.'

At last, they had all the fake jewels sewn on to the costumes and the real ones lying in a glittering pile on

May's headscarf. May knotted it tight around them and put it into the plastic bag in which she had brought her sandwiches. She threw the empty lunch-box in on top of them and hung the bag on the hook behind the door, underneath her jacket.

Light was flooding in through the dusty window, and the clock bells from Dublin Castle, St. Patrick's and Christ Church Cathedrals chimed out seven o'clock. May hung the costumes back in the press, locked it and put the key in the pocket of her jeans. Imelda yawned and sank back in her chair.

'There'll be no one here for ages,' she said. 'We can get some shut-eye.'

'I dunno,' May said uneasily. 'You wanna be outa here before Scruffy gets in. You don't have to be in for anything this morning, and she'd be dead suspicious if she found you here.'

'I'll go home and get a proper kip as soon as the front's open,' Imelda declared. 'But I dunno how yer gonna keep goin' all day?'

'Nor do I,' May admitted. 'I'm jaded. But you can't stay up here till they open the box-office.'

'O.K. I'll shift later.' Imelda's eyes were closed.

May looked at her in panic. Once asleep they might never wake until Scruffy was in on top of them. Then she had an idea.

'The couch for Act One!' she said. 'The stage hands set up Act One before they left. We can both sleep on stage. We'll hear them comin' in from there and wake before anyone puts the lights on.'

Imelda was reluctant to move but the couch sounded a lot more comfortable than the hard Wardrobe chairs.

'Come on then,' she said.

They groped their way in darkness round the backcloth and through the gap between the black velvet curtains.

'Take care,' May warned. 'We don't wanna fall into the orchestra pit and break our necks.'

'It's O.K.,' said Imelda. 'The couch is well upstage and there's nothing else to fall over.'

She had hardly spoken when something hit her.

'What's wrong?' May called anxiously.

'I just walked into a step-ladder, that's all! Someone musta put it there just to spite me.'

Then she tripped over the couch and fell sprawling across it. With a sigh of content, she lay still and slept. Stretching out beside her, May slept too.

When she opened her eyes, Nick was standing looking down on her. She struggled to a sitting position, her mind fighting against sleep. What explanation could she possibly give?

'And what d'you imagine you're doing?' he asked.

'I came in early because Sylvia's costume got awful crumpled last night and I wanted to give it a press,' May lied desperately. 'Only the Wardrobe was locked so I thought I'd lie down here till Mrs. Mullen got in and I musta dozed off!'

She waited for a question about Imelda, racking her brain for some story, but all he said was:

'If I find you've touched any of the props you know what'll happen to your friend. Now get the hell out of here!'

She struggled to her feet and, glancing at the couch, saw only a heap of goatskins heside her. Imelda must

83

have pulled them on top of her, completely covering herself. But Nick might discover her at any moment. She hesitated, wondering how she could get Nick out of the way until she could wake Imelda.

'I told you to get out of here!' Nick said.

Just then the designer's face appeared round the corner of the backcloth:

'Jimmy! Could you come here for a minute?'

The second he was out of sight, May clapped a hand over Imelda's mouth and shook her, praying that she was not too sleepy to take in her words.

'Quick!' she whispered. 'Wake up! Nick's here!'

To her relief, she saw Imelda's eyes open wide and she was on her feet in an instant.

'This way,' May whispered, and they both ran down the passage away from the scene dock. The stage doorman was standing in the open office doorway, talking to the girl inside. Imelda did not hesitate, but pushed open the door and slipped out into the lane. The doorman turned at the sound of the door closing.

'Who went out?' he asked May.

'The designer,' May lied. 'I think she went to get something outa her car.'

Satisfied, he turned back and continued his conversation as May hurried up to the Wardrobe. Mrs. Mullen and Scruffy were already there, fussing over the costumes, and May found she was indeed expected to iron Sylvia's costumes once more.

By seven-thirty that night she was going through the routine of the day before like a robot and it was only when she met Maura on the stairs that she remembered to wish her good luck.

'Just forget about the audience,' she said. But Maura only gave a tight little smile and went on down the stairs.

When May reached the stage she suddenly became aware of a buzz of voices on the other side of the front curtain. Imelda pointed to a small hole cut into them at eye level, and when she peeped through it she saw people crowding in through the doors on either side. Then the orchestra struck up the overture.

In the wings, Richie and Mickser were waiting.

'Well done,' Richie whispered softly as she passed.

'Did Melly tell you that Nick saw me?' she whispered.

Richie nodded: 'You got away with it, but...'

'I dunno,' May said. 'He's awful suspicious. I hope he doesn't try anything.'

'We'll be ready for him if he does,' Richie said. 'We've brought down our gear so we can change outa costume between the battle scene and the Act 1 finale, so we can slip out front if we have to.'

Five minutes later, standing against the back wall, May heard the whirr of the great curtain rising. She set Sylvia's armour out ready and waited.

Roger and Sylvia were singing their counting song. Suddenly May heard a sound she had never heard before; a distant ripple of laughter that spread around the theatre and swelled into a great roar. Sylvia must have pulled out the golden chamber-pot from under the couch. May glanced over to where Maura stood, waiting for her entrance. She looked taut as a fiddle-string. How could she forget, hearing that roar, the people out there watching?

Out of the corner of her eye, May suddenly saw Nick up on the cat-walk, close to the flood that would be directly over Maura's head. Was it just chance or did he mean to carry out his threat?

Without waiting to work it out, May ran for the stairs and, within seconds, was between him and the flood. Then he seized her shoulders in a vice-like grip and pushed her forward against the fly-rail.

'Now,' he said. 'Why was your friend Imelda here this morning?'

'I don't know what you're talkin' about!' May lied desperately. She could see Roger and Sylvia far below her on the stage. They had reached the end of their song. It was time for Maura's entrance.

'She was seen leaving the theatre just after I found you asleep on the couch. You were both here all night, weren't you?'

May shook her head wordlessly.

'Weren't you?' Nick repeated, forcing her body out over the fly-rail so that her feet swung clear of the cat-walk. 'Answer me or I'll let go,' he said softly.

A wave of sickness flooded over her. The stage hung below her at a crazy angle.

'Yes! yes! We were here,' she sobbed.

'Why?' he demanded. 'What were the two of you at?'

She had no fight left in her. What was the use?. She was about to tell him everything when suddenly she felt arms about her waist. She was being dragged back over the fly-rail. She heard a thud as a fist struck Nick's body. Richie and Mickser had arrived. Then she was lying in a tangled heap on the cat-walk.

Lying there in a daze, she became aware of Maura's voice, soaring up from below. In a few minutes, Sylvia would be coming off stage for her quick change. She could never manage it on her own. May stumbled back down the stairs, leaving the boys still struggling on the cat-walk with Nick.

As she hurried to where she had left the armour, she saw Maura on stage, raising the cloak. As her voice died away there was a rattle of applause. Maura had got an exit round! May wanted to go to her and hug her but there was no time. There was a much bigger burst of applause and then Sylvia was beside her. May helped her into the armour, zipping the tunic closed without a hitch, and then Sylvia was striding back on stage once more.

Feeling faint, May looked up at the fly-rail. It was empty! Nick was nowhere to be seen. It was as if she had dreamed the whole thing. In a daze, she collected Sylvia's opening costume and set off for the dressing-rooms.

As the curtain came down on Act 1, everyone was chattering excitedly about how the show was going, but Richie silently grabbed her by the arm and pulled her into the window alcove at the top of the stairs.

'We can't wait till the end of the show now!' he said urgently. 'You gotta get the jewels to Linda's grandfather at once!'

8   And The Curtain Falls

May looked at Richie in alarm: 'But Linda and her grand-dad won't be comin' backstage till after the show, and I can't go out front while it's on!'

'Yer the only one not in costume now,' Richie argued. 'We'd never have time to change and be ready again for the start of Act II. The interval's fifteen minutes. If you go quick you'll easy do it.'

'But they'll never let me go!' May told him.

'So don't ask them,' Richie said, and ran off after the others. Once again, it seemed, everything depended on May. She slipped into the Wardrobe and found Mrs. Mullen and Scruffy both there.

'Sylvia somehow managed to catch her hem on something,' Mrs. Mullen told her, 'and it's all ripped. Would you ever leave back Roger's opening costume for Betty while she fixes it?'

'Of course!' May cried, delighted. It was a gift!

She grabbed the plastic bag and her jacket off the hook behind the door, heaped Roger's costume on top of them and hurried out. She tapped on Roger's dressing-room door and he opened it himself.

'Betty asked me to leave these back,' she said. 'Where do they go?' and she started towards the row of hooks on the wall.

'I'll see to them,' Roger said. He took them from her, and May thought yet again that if the tall actor was conceited, he was also very kind and helpful. Then, slipping on her jacket she hurried downstairs.

She tapped on the door of the office and, when there was no reply, looked in. It was empty. The management was out front with the audience. She ran in one door and out the other into the sloping passage beyond. The swing doors leading into the auditorium were tied back and May slipped through them, unnoticed amongst the women on their way out to the *Ladies*.

She had worried about finding Linda and her grandfather amongst all those people, but most of them seemed to have gone to one or the other of the two bars at the back of the stalls, and she spotted them easily in the middle of row J. Hurriedly she explained as best she could what had happened and thrust the plastic bag into the old man's hands.

'I'll go at once,' he told her, rising from his seat. 'Tell the others to take no risks during the second half. Linda, you stay here!' and he set off for the exit.

'Maura was wonderful,' Linda told May. 'Please tell her so from me and tell her to take care.'

Out of the corner of her eye, May saw the front-of-house manager in evening dress, coming from the back of the stalls. She felt conspicuous in her jeans, with most of the women dolled up in smart dresses for the opening of the show.

'I must go,' she said. 'See you later!' and she darted out into the passage, back through the office and up the stairs to arrive panting, in the Wardrobe. As she checked the things that had to be done during the second half of the show, she heard Phil's voice over the Tannoy calling:

'Act Two beginners, please!'

The second half was going splendidly. The audience seemed really excited by the battle scenes — even standing backstage May could feel the tense silence in which they watched them; and the big chorus number describing the contest between the two bulls, which Richie, Mickser and Imelda had rehearsed for so long, brought the house down, with cheering and foot-stamping as well as clapping. The show was a success,

89

she thought happily, as she ran upstairs to fetch Sylvia's cloak for the final curtain.

As she reached the open door of the Wardrobe on her way to Sylvia's dressing-room, she heard an angry cry and Scruffy burst from the room, barring her way. In her hand, she held the empty cardboard box in which she had kept the fake jewels.

'Were you at this box?' she yelled at May.

May felt a shiver go through her. What was the point in denying it? Nick would guess the truth at once. She nodded her head.

'Where are the stones?' Scruffy screamed.

'Back on the costumes,' May faltered.

Scruffy's eyes blazed and she moved towards May as if she would claw her eyes out. Then Maura and the actress who played Emer suddenly came out of their dressing-room. The only two not on stage for the last two scenes, they had now to wait in the wings, ready to take their places for the curtain calls. With a look of helpless fury, Scruffy turned away and ran down the stairs ahead of her. She had almost certainly gone to tell Nick, May thought, but cheered herself up with the knowledge that Maura's scenes were all over and no harm could come to her now.

She went on to Sylvia's dressing-room, collected the cloak and stood with it in the prompt corner, waiting. Then, amid thunderous applause that drowned the whirr of its machinery, the great front curtain fell and an elated Sylvia stood by her side. May clasped her cloak around her shoulders as she moved upstage, ready to re-enter from the back into the centre of the line-up.

She could see Nick, standing by to cue the curtain up

again. He could do nothing now, she thought. The cast were all crowding on to the stage to take up the positions Jane had given them, except for Sylvia, Roger and the actors who played Cúchulainn, Conor and Fergus. They were standing waiting, two men on either side, ready to go on after the curtain was up, with Sylvia who would come on last by herself. The applause was still going on and seemed to May to be almost deafening.

The curtain rose again and the half-circle bowed. May looked across to where Maura stood near the far end of the curve. Her face was no longer white, but flushed with excitement and happiness. Then a sudden movement above drew May's eyes upwards and she saw a figure moving purposefully along the cat-walk. As the curtain fell once more, cutting out the strong beams from the front-of-house spotlights that dazzled her eyes, May suddenly knew from his heavy build and the unusually long arms that the man was the Slasher. Then the curtain rose again and the strong shafts of light plunged him into darkness once more.

Terror seized May. The whole width of the stage lay between her and the stairs up to the fly-rail. Could she get to the Slasher in time to prevent him from doing whatever ghastly thing he had in mind? By now she knew he must be almost above where Maura was standing.

The principals were coming on now as the applause rose to a crescendo, and May realized it was loud enough to cover any noise the Slasher might make. The thought had hardly occurred to her when she thought she heard a faint cry and, as Sylvia took her place in the centre of the half-circle, bowing, and the curtain fell again, she

91

began to run. Right across the stage behind the startled cast she streaked, reaching the foot of the stairs as the curtain began to rise again. Hurling herself up the stairs, her breath catching in her throat and her heart pounding, she looked up to where she knew Slasher must be, but the rising curtain once again plunged the area into darkness. Then, as she reached the top of the stairs, the curtain fell again and she saw him plainly, right in front of her. He was struggling in the grip of a burly garda, who held him pinioned from behind. May sat down on the edge of the cat-walk and burst into tears.

No one felt quite right having a party that night, with Nick and Scruffy held for questioning and the props taken away for examination by the gardaí, but everyone agreed it would be unfair to Jane and Sylvia not to go. The party was only being held in one of the theatre bars, but when Maura saw the gorgeous dress Sylvia had brought to wear for it she felt like going home. Phil soon talked her out of that though.

'You can't possibly go straight home after an opening,' she said. 'You need to unwind. Besides, you've got to celebrate our success!'

'You'd better wait till we see what the critics have to say in the papers tomorrow before calling it a success,' Jane said, overhearing Phil's last words. But even she agreed that the audience had seemed to love the show.

'Don't stay up too late though,' she told Phil. 'You and I are going to have to have a crisis meeting at ten tomorrow.'

Phil nodded. She would have to get official permission to borrow what they needed from the Abbey Theatre, check everything was there and arrange transport. And even if the gardaí released Nick on bail, Jane felt it would be unwise to let him run the show.

She asked Phil anxiously if she thought she would be able to manage provided she had extra help, and was surprised at how calmly she took it.

'You didn't tell her I'd warned you to be ready to take over, did you,' Maura asked nervously.

'Of course not!' Phil said. 'Wasn't it much better for me to let her think I'm just naturally good in a crisis?'

So Maura went to the party, even though she had only her jeans to wear, and Phil also went in jeans just to keep her company. Whacker was there too by special invitation, as well as Linda and her grandfather who had come round backstage after the show like Maura had told them to do, just as the squad car left with Slasher, Nick, Scruffy and the props.

As May said, the only person who was missing was old Danny Noonan, but when she told Jane about him and how he had told her the real story of the *Táin*, Jane gave her a little bottle of something and a few goodies wrapped in a paper napkin to take home to him.

It was a good party and, even though no one from the Square stayed until the end, none of them got to bed till the small hours. For once, Maura's mother let her sleep on and she only woke when the rest of the gang arrived on the doorstep. Whacker's father had given him the money to go out and buy all the morning papers and, as soon as they had read what was written about the show, Whacker and Imelda collected May, Richie and Mickser and they all went round to Maura's house.

Maura could not believe her eyes when she read the papers. Not only had the critics loved the show but two of them mentioned her by name. One listed her with some of the others as giving good support, but one welcomed her as a promising newcomer whose future should be worth watching.

'She'll be givin' herself great airs now,' said Imelda, a small bit jealous if the truth must be told.

'Of course she won't,' scoffed May. 'Maura isn't like that!'

'We'll all be boastin' we knew her when she had nothing,' Richie grinned, almost as pleased as Maura was herself, and Whacker summed it all up when he said:

'Maybe one day we'll even be watchin' her on the telly!'

Patchie made a funny sort of snorting noise just then and Maura laughed.

'Patchie thinks that's ridiculous, don't you, Patch?' she said, but May shook her head.

'It's only that he's fed up with us all doin' something he can't do with us,' she said.

Maura patted the little black patch that gave him his name and kissed the tip of his little wet nose.

'Don't you mind them, Patchie ould son,' she said. 'When I'm famous I'll play Peg in *Peg O' My Heart* and I won't have any dog only you in the part of Peg's dog, Michael!'

Theatre Terms

Cat-walk or fly-rail: The narrow passage that runs around three sides of, and high above the stage, protected only by a light rail.

Floods: Short for flood-lights, which flood a large area of the stage with light, unlike the spotlights, which can be focussed so as to light the face of one performer only.

Gels: Short for gelatines, the squares cut from rolls of stiff, transparent coloured material like film negative, to fit into metal frames which slide over the front of flood or spotlights in order to make the light amber, blue, pink and so on instead of pure white.

Prompt corner: The corner of the stage out of sight of the audience, where the prompter stands, following the action taking place on stage with the help of the prompt book. In this is written the dialogue so that if anyone on stage forgets a line (or 'dries' as this is called) the prompter can call it out.

Proscenium arch: The frame through which the audience sees the action on stage, which is closed off when the front curtains are lowered.

Straight juv. make-up: Juv. is short for juvenile, or young, and 'straight' means to look as you are, unlike 'character' make-up, which is intended to make you look older or give you the characteristic features of another race or the appearance of, say, a witch or a ghost.

Carolyn Swift

Carolyn Swift has worked in most Dublin theatres, including the Olympia, either as actress, stage-manager or producer, and for ten years ran a small theatre in partnership with her husband. For the stage she wrote seven revues, a rock musical and puppet plays, as well as plays and series for radio and television, including *Wanderly Wagon, Bosco* and *Fortycoats.*

She is a regular contributer to Radio Éireann's Sunday morning programme, *Sunday Miscellany.*

Her first three books for The Children's Press, *Robbers in the House, Robbers in the Hills,* and *Robbers in the Town* were dedicated to her three daughters.